WE RESIST

Scott P Overmyer, PhD

ISBN: 979-8-90405-111-2

Dedication

This book is dedicated to my wife of 47 years, whose strength and patience carried us through everything, and to my children, who grew into remarkable adults—largely because of her.

Acknowledgment

I owe a deep debt of gratitude to my wife, whose patience, strength, and steady presence made this book—and much else in my life - possible. For nearly five decades, she has borne more than her share without complaint, and I am more grateful than words can convey.

To my children, thank you for your understanding over the years and for growing into the kind of people any parent would be proud of. Watching who you've become has been one of the great privileges of my life.

My time at TRW Inc. first introduced me to the complex and often unseen world of government systems—how they function, how they fail, and how they can be bent in ways most people never see.

To those who have served—especially in roles that are rarely seen or fully understood—your experiences and sacrifices helped shape the spirit of this story.

And finally, to the readers: thank you for taking the time to step into this world. I hope the story challenges you, stays with you, and perhaps even makes you look at things a little differently.

About the Author

Dr. Scott P. Overmyer began his career in software engineering in 1983 with TRW Inc., working on government systems at the Cheyenne Mountain Complex. That early experience helped shape the technical and thematic foundation for We Resist.

He later earned a Ph.D. in Information Technology while serving as a Research Instructor at George Mason University Center of Excellence in Command, Control, Communications, and Intelligence.

Dr. Overmyer brings nearly 10 years of industry experience and more than 30 years in academia. His career includes research fellowships at the NASA Johnson Space Center, leadership roles on National Science Foundation grants, and faculty positions at Drexel University, Massey University, and Nazarbayev University.

He is currently an Instructional Assistant Professor at Illinois State University and previously served as Associate Dean for Information Technology programs at Southern New Hampshire University.

His current interests include artificial intelligence, human-computer interaction, and—when time permits—poker and winemaking.

Table of Contents

Chapter One: The Breaking Point

The drone passed in four seconds. Avril counted without thinking—four seconds meant facial scan, license plates, maybe a sweep of open wireless signals. Last month, it had been six. He didn't look up from the window.

Outside, the street was the same as always. A man walking a dog. A woman in a yellow coat is checking her phone. Two kids on bikes were weaving around a pothole the city had been ignoring for a year. Normal life, going through its motions. The drone slid behind the skyline and was gone.

Avril turned back to his screen. The feeds were running, same as every morning: three aggregators, two message boards, a scrape of court filing databases that updated hourly. He'd built the monitoring stack over eight months, layering it the way you layered defenses, each tool compensating for another's blind spots. The stack had its own rhythm now — the particular pulse of a city under persistent low-grade surveillance, the gaps and spikes that told you something was happening before the official channels admitted it. He'd learned to read it the way old sailors read weather: not from instruments, from the quality of the air.

A new flag in the court filings: three emergency protective orders filed in the same district and week by the same employer. A flag on one of the message boards: a school district in Ohio quietly removed a reading curriculum that included first-person accounts of the internment camps. Small things. The kind that didn't make the news cycle because, individually, they didn't add up to a story. Together, they were something else. He kept the running total in a notebook, one line per entry, no interpretation. Interpretation was what you did when you had enough entries. He was still counting.

The apartment was small and had been smaller since Lena left, not because she'd taken much, but because silence takes up space. That had been two years ago. He still caught himself reaching for the second coffee mug some mornings.

He wasn't thinking about her now. He was thinking about a twenty-three-second video.

He'd downloaded it in the twelve minutes before it was scrubbed from every platform simultaneously—a coordination that still kept him up some nights. In it, a young woman stood outside a bookstore, holding a hand-lettered sign with a quote from the Constitution above a hand-drawn dove. Two men in black gear approached. She turned to walk away. They took her anyway, professional and quick, and a black van materialized at the curb like it had been waiting all morning. As the doors closed, she called out her name— "Lina Alvarez! I'm not resisting!"— and then the van was gone, and the people on the street slowly lowered their phones.

He spent three days finding out who she was.

Lina Alvarez. Twenty-seven. Civics teacher, community organizer, daughter of an undocumented mother who'd spent most of her life making herself invisible. Lina had not inherited that instinct. She ran mutual aid networks during the food shortages and organized neighborhood watches when federal contractors began making "random visits." She published a digital zine documenting illegal detentions—mostly of teenagers—featuring hand-drawn sketches, audio logs, and a careful, damning list of the security subcontractors involved. She wasn't trying to take anyone down. She was trying to make people see.

She'd grown up in Eastside Borough, knowing fear but refusing to live by it. Her strength wasn't loud—it was the kind that showed up with rice and beans and a flashlight when the power went out, that looked you in the eye when everyone else had learned to look away. Two months before she was taken, she gave a talk at a public library: bad lighting, worse audio. Avril listened to it four times.

"They want us to forget each other. That's how they win. Not with tanks. With silence. Memory loss. But we're still here. I see you."

He sat in the dark for an hour after that, then opened a new tab. He typed the name three times before letting it stand. He deleted the first two — not because they were wrong, but because seeing it on the screen made it real in a way it hadn't been in his head, and real meant traceable, and traceable meant consequences for people who might not have chosen to be involved. He sat with the blinking cursor for another ten minutes. He became aware of his hands on the keyboard. They were not entirely steady. He thought about Lina Alvarez saying her name into the closing van doors — not for the people watching, he'd decided, but for herself. So the record would have it. So the record would know. He hit the post.

We Resist. Black screen, white Courier font. No graphics, no trackers, no ads. Just: this happened. He posted the Lina video first. Then a write-up about a neighbor taken during the night. Then, archived links, whistleblower threads, blurry photos shot from high-rise windows. He set up rotating mirror links through VPNs in Iceland, Brazil, and Taiwan, the way you'd plan an escape route before you knew you'd need one.

The first morning: three views.

The second night: ten.

End of week: five thousand, and climbing. Somewhere on the second day, he'd crossed a line he couldn't identify precisely but could feel in retrospect. Before it: documentation, which he'd told himself was neutral. After it: a site with a name and a purpose and five thousand people who'd found their way to it. Documentation didn't have a name. We Resist did. A name meant you were claiming something — that these things happened, that they were connected, that someone was keeping the account. He understood the difference now in a way he hadn't when he'd registered the domain at three in the morning, half-convinced he was doing something small. He hadn't been doing something small. He hadn't been doing something small at all.

He hadn't left the apartment in four days. Lena would have had something to say about that. She used to tell him he was disappearing from the inside out — not broken, just choosing to watch everything burn and call it staying informed. He remembered the last morning in particular: her standing in the kitchen doorway in the gray light, coat already on, a mug in both hands, one she'd stopped pretending to drink from. She hadn't said anything new. She'd said his name once, the way you say a name when you want someone to look up from the screen and be in the room with you.

The way a teacher says a name. The way someone says a name when they're asking a question they've already answered for themselves, but need you to answer too. He hadn't looked up. He'd understood what she meant and hadn't known how to change it, and eventually she'd stopped waiting for him to figure it out. He didn't blame her. Some part of him had been relieved, which he blamed himself for more than the leaving itself. The relief meant something he didn't want to examine — that he'd wanted the apartment to himself, the screens to himself, the uninterrupted hours of pulling at threads without anyone asking him to stop. That he'd wanted to disappear from the inside out, and she'd been in the way. He wasn't sure that was better than what he'd told himself at the time.

He was different now. Or he was doing something different, at least. He wasn't sure yet if those were the same thing.

The Signal message had come in three days after he posted Lina's video. No metadata. Six relays. Just:

We believe in what you're doing. We can help. Former JSOC. Not just tech. We do ops.

He hadn't answered. Not because he thought it was a honeypot—though it might be—but because he understood what answering would mean. JSOC wasn't rhetoric. It was people who went into black sites that didn't officially exist, who'd spent careers believing in the machine and were now, apparently, watching it become something else. If this were real, it meant the erosion had gone deep enough to shake loose people who'd once been its instrument.

The cursor blinked in the reply field. Outside, the muffled thrum of another drone moved across the window and faded.

He wasn't a fighter. He still got nervous making phone calls. But he knew how to listen, how to find patterns in noise, how to move information through firewalls and make it mean something on the other side. He'd spent two years getting very good at it while telling himself it didn't count as doing anything.

He put his hands on the keyboard.

Maybe that was the problem with the story he'd been telling himself—that someone like him needed to wait for someone else to start.

Chapter Two: First Contact

Avril hadn't moved in forty-seven minutes.

The message still glowed on the screen. Three words back, three words forward — Prove you're real — and now silence on both ends. He'd typed it fast, before he could think better of it, and hit send the way you jump from a height before your body registers what you're doing.

He stood and paced. Five steps wall to wall. His apartment was barely the size of a large conference room — no hallway, no coat closet, the bed practically part of the kitchen. He'd never minded before. Now it felt like a cell he'd built himself.

The logic was simple, which was the problem. Either the message was real — former JSOC, actual capabilities, people who'd served the machine and were now watching it become something else — or it was a honeypot. The patient is kind. Not designed for radicals and brick-throwers but for the quiet ones, the archivists, the people who connected dots in the dark and called it not doing anything.

He scrubbed his system. Rerouted traffic, wiped cache, checked VPN integrity. His fingers moved through the commands out of habit more than logic. If they were already coming, this was theater.

He brewed coffee. Burnt it. Didn't drink it.

Two hours passed. Then three. Signal sat open on the screen, untouched, as a note slipped under a door he wasn't sure led anywhere.

At 3:17 a.m., he heard a vehicle pull up outside.

Not unusual. Not in the city. But it didn't move. Just idled.

He went to the window slowly, peeled back the curtain a sliver.

Black van. No markings. Tinted windows.

He didn't reach for the go-bag — not yet. He just stood there, watching it the way you watch a dog you're not sure about. Five minutes. Ten. His breath had gone shallow without him noticing.

Then the van drove off. No one got out. No one came in.

He exhaled, but it wasn't relief — it was pressure bleeding out of the cracks. He knew it was possible the van hadn't been for him. Just a contractor. Or surveillance on someone else. Or Lina's van had looked exactly like that, too, sliding up to the curb as it belonged there, doors closing on a scream.

He didn't sleep. He sat in his chair, half-alert, half-hollow, and waited.

At 4:51 a.m., his phone vibrated once.

Fair. You'll get proof. Wait for contact. 24-48 hours, not over this channel.

– Null

He reread it five times. Null. A placeholder. An absence. Or just someone who understood that names were liabilities.

He lay down on the couch without taking his shoes off, staring at the ceiling while the laptop blinked across the room. Forty-eight hours, he told himself. He could hold it together for forty-eight hours.

Lena would've laughed at that. Not cruelly — she wasn't cruel — but with the particular tired affection of someone who'd watched him white-knuckle through things that didn't require white-knuckling. You treat waiting like it's something you have to survive, she'd said once. Like, stillness is going to kill you.

He'd thought about that a lot after she left. He still wasn't sure she was wrong.

He slept in one-hour shifts. Fully clothed.

The sticker appeared on the second morning.

Small. About the size of a quarter. Red, circular, stuck to the outside of his door frame, low enough to miss if you weren't looking. He hadn't put it there. It hadn't been there the night before. The hallway camera had glitched at 2:40 a.m. — a half-second stutter, one skipped frame — and then resumed as if nothing had happened.

He stood staring at it for a long moment, then took a photo and went back inside without touching it.

Twenty minutes later, the countdown he'd been running in his head hit zero. He checked Signal. Nothing. Checked the laptop. Nothing.

Then he checked under the doormat.

A plain white envelope. No address, no stamp. Inside, a single sheet of printer paper, monospaced font, one sentence:

3:15 PM. 86th & Halstead. Northwest bench. Black hoodie. No tech.

He checked the clock. Ninety-three minutes.

He stood at the window for a moment, watching the street below—a mail truck. A neighbor's cat was moving along the sidewalk with the calm authority of something that owned the block. A delivery guy with a dolly full of water jugs.

Normal life, same as always. He used to find that comforting.

He got dressed and left.

He arrived at 3:08 and spent the first minute across the street, watching from the mouth of a bodega doorway with a bottle of water he'd bought to have a reason to stand there. At 3:10, a man in a black hoodie sat down on the bench—average height. Athletic build. Avril felt his pulse kick and made himself wait rather than cross. He watched for thirty seconds. The man took out his phone, tilted it toward the sun, and frowned at the screen. Texted something. The particular body language of someone killing time. Not him. Avril exhaled slowly and stayed where he was until 3:12, when the man got up and caught a bus. He crossed the street, sat on the bench — left side, same as he always did on the subway; he didn't want to give them anything new to read — and told himself the pulse kick had been useful information. Not fear. Just calibration. His body was registering what his mind was still negotiating. He still hadn't entirely stopped shaking by 3:14.

Black hoodie, no tech, clean sneakers, a folded bill in his back pocket for bus fare. He'd left his phone at home, powered off, wrapped in foil, inside an old coffee can. He felt strangely light without it. Unmoored. Like a man who'd forgotten his own name.

The northwest bench was a narrow stretch of concrete with a battered wooden seat facing a bus stop no one really used. A cigarette still smoldered in the tray beside it. Scuff marks on the ground. Someone had been here recently.

At 3:14, a figure came out of the alley across the street. Average height, athletic build, black hoodie, head down. Moving at the particular pace of someone who'd been trained not to look like they were moving with purpose.

They sat on the other end of the bench—six feet between them. Neither looked directly at the other.

The contact spoke first—a male voice, flat and neutral, with the cadence of someone delivering information rather than having a conversation.

"You were watched. You weren't followed."

Avril said nothing.

"We've been on your site since the first week. Took us a while to confirm you weren't a plant." A beat. "Your exit node routing — you're cycling through the same three in a pattern. Every third post, same sequence. You probably don't know you're doing it." He turned something over in his fingers — a coin, or a washer, Avril couldn't tell. A habit. The kind you don't know you have. "We'll fix it." "You've been watching my posting patterns." "We watch everything. That's the job." He said it without apology or emphasis, the tone of someone stating a physical law. "Yours are better than most. Which means whoever's watching from the other direction has been watching for a while too, and they've had more time to map the pattern than we have." Another beat. "Something to think about."

"Why me?" Avril asked.

The man was quiet for a moment. A bus roared past and blotted out the city.

"Because you're documenting. Not performing." He turned the coin again. "There are a lot of people right now who want to be seen resisting. You want the resistance actually to work. That's different. That's useful."

He stood. Didn't look at Avril directly, even then.

"Location drop tonight. Twenty-four hours to verify. After that, you meet the rest. Come alone. No devices. Don't improvise." A pause. "If you don't show, you drop off our grid. No second contact."

He walked off without waiting for a response and folded back into the city the way water closes around a stone.

Avril stayed on the bench for another full minute, watching the street. The mail truck was gone. The cat was gone. The delivery guy, the kid on the scooter, the woman with the stroller — all of it cycling through its ordinary business, indifferent and endless.

He thought about Lina Alvarez standing outside a bookstore with a hand-drawn dove, believing in the visibility of ordinary things.

Then he stood, turned in the opposite direction, and walked back the way he'd come. He was two blocks from his building when he noticed the delivery guy. Same man. Same dolly. Same stack of water jugs, still undelivered. Standing at the corner of 84th and Mercer with his back to the street, apparently studying the label on one of the jugs with the careful attention of someone who was not, in any meaningful sense, studying the label on a water jug. Avril didn't slow down. Didn't change direction. He kept the same pace, turned at his usual corner, went through his building's side entrance, and stood in the stairwell for a full two minutes before going upstairs.

The man might have been nothing. A slow route. A bored contractor. The city was full of people who looked like something from one angle and something else entirely from another. He had no way to know. That was the thing he was going to have to learn to live with: no way to know. The contact had said you were watched, you weren't followed, and Avril had understood in the moment that this was reassurance. He understood now, standing in a stairwell with his hand on the rail, that it was also a warning.

They watched everything. That was the job. It was everyone's job now — every side, every angle, every delivery guy at every corner. The question wasn't whether you were being watched. The question was whether the person watching you was on your side or someone else's, and most of the time, you would not know the answer until it was too late for the answer to matter.

He went upstairs. He made coffee. He sat at the table and looked at the blank Signal screen and thought about exit nodes cycling in patterns he hadn't known he was making, and all the other patterns he was making that he hadn't noticed yet. He didn't sleep for a long time.

Chapter Three: Lines in the Sand

The basement apartment smelled like old concrete and someone else's decisions. Avril had been there three days — borrowed space, borrowed time — and he still hadn't put anything on the walls except a fiber map covered in pins and red thread. It felt like a war room that hadn't decided what war it was fighting yet.

His laptop fan buzzed. On screen: five feeds, five faces, five people who'd each found their own reasons to end up here.

He'd been studying them for two minutes before anyone spoke.

Carrick filled the upper-left frame the way certain men fill a room — not loudly, just completely. Arms crossed, metal folding chair, the posture of someone who'd learned to sleep anywhere and trust no one. "Former Tier One," he said. "I don't do politics. I do results. We clear?"

Avril said yes. Carrick didn't look convinced.

The woman next to him on screen — Major Elena Soto, retired, five continents — had a stillness to her that wasn't calm so much as controlled. She studied Avril the way you study a map before a crossing. Looking for where the ground might give.

Wrecker was in the lower left, slouched in a hoodie, jaw working like he was chewing something he'd already swallowed. He hadn't introduced himself — Mason had done it for him.

Wrecker breaks things, Mason had said. Sometimes people. He'll grow on you. Wrecker had said nothing to confirm or deny this.

Mason himself was the warmest face on the call, which Avril was already learning not to take at face value. The room behind him was too sterile. Weapons on the pegboard. Maps without country names. His smile reached his eyes, but his eyes were doing something else entirely.

"You found my site," Avril said to him.

"First week," Mason said. "Told these cynics you were worth a look. That was a gamble on my part. I'd like it to pay off."

Carrick leaned forward. "You want to be part of this. Fine. But intel gets people killed if it's wrong. You got sources, or you got headlines?"

"Both," Avril said. "And I verify before I amplify. Every time."

"Easy to say."

"I know." Avril kept his voice level. "I'm not asking you to trust me yet. I'm asking you to let me show you how I work."

Soto spoke for the first time. "What happens when your conscience says no and our mission says yes?"

"Then we argue," Avril said. "And if we can't get there, I walk. I won't compromise the mission — or myself — to stay in the room." He paused. "But I don't think that's why you brought me here. A conscience isn't useful if it folds."

Soto said nothing. But something in her expression shifted, just slightly, the way a door shifts when the latch releases.

He hadn't planned what came next. It came out of him the way things do when you've been carrying them too long.

"I used to believe this country corrected its mistakes," he said. "That if you pulled back the curtain, people would care. That truth was enough."

Nobody moved. Even Wrecker had stopped chewing.

"But what broke me wasn't just the government. It was watching how many people liked what it became. Coworkers. Friends. My aunt. The guy I used to coach Little League with — good man, fundraised for cancer research, drove kids to practice.

He watched them drag a woman into a van on the news and said she probably had it coming." Avril looked at the screen. "I kept waiting for someone to say this isn't who we are. Turns out it is. Enough of us to matter."

The silence that followed was different from before. Less evaluation. More recognition.

"So, if I'm risking everything," he said, quieter now, "it's going to be for something better than that."

—

The next hour turned philosophical in the way that only happens when soldiers and civilians find themselves on the same side of a line they didn't expect to cross together.

They needed a protocol. Not rules — rules were for organizations that trusted their own bureaucracies — but a set of shared limits, things they'd each be willing to be held to. Avril pushed for it. Carrick resisted. "Unanimous consent on ops." He said it back flatly, like reading an absurdity aloud. "You know what unanimous consent looks like in a field situation? It looks like someone is dying while the committee meets." "We're not in the field yet," Avril said. "We will be. And when we are, this protocol of yours is going to get someone killed because someone with principles couldn't make a call." "Or it stops someone with a gun from making a call they'll spend the rest of their life trying to unmake."

Avril held his gaze. "Which is why you're here and not still in whatever you walked away from." The silence stretched long enough that Soto glanced at Carrick's feed. He had the expression of a man who had picked something up and was deciding whether to put it down or throw it. Then he set it down. Not because he'd been persuaded — the jaw said he hadn't — but because something in what Avril said had landed somewhere specific. "Fine," he said. "We do it your way. First time it costs us, we revisit." "Fair," Avril said. It was the first thing Carrick had said that wasn't a challenge or a test. Avril understood it as a different kind of test entirely.

Truth over narrative. Evidence vetted before action. Purpose over punishment — target the operation, not the person.

No op that risks civilian lives without unanimous consent. Leaks before violence, always. No personal gain, ever.

"And who decides?" Carrick asked.

"All of us. Unanimous."

Carrick looked like he wanted to argue, then didn't. "That's going to be slow."

"It's supposed to be," Avril said.

Soto leaned back. "Paper rules break easily. What matters is who you are when everything goes wrong. So." She looked around the call. "When did you have to choose?"

Carrick went first. In Somalia, a warlord, aid workers unknowingly provide cover. He'd leaked their names to get them pulled out before he understood the full picture. Two of them never went back to the field. He'd lived with that.

Soto: Venezuela. A commander using food distribution as a loyalty test, letting people starve for the camera, and calling it relief. She'd smuggled out footage. It was extracted forty-eight hours later. Lost her rank, kept her conscience.

Mason: Belarus. Students are being surveilled by their own university. He'd slipped the counter-surveillance tools through a dead drop. Three got out. He'd lost his clearance and gained, he said, considerably better sleep. He smiled when he said it — warm, self-deprecating, the smile of a man who had made peace with the cost. It was exactly the right response. It landed exactly the way a carefully calibrated response lands. Avril found himself watching Mason's eyes again. They were doing the same thing they'd been doing since the call started: receiving information, filing it, revealing nothing.

The smile was real. The warmth was probably real. But there was a layer beneath it that processed everything it was given without showing the processing, and Avril had enough experience with people who needed to be liked to know the difference between that and someone who was likeable. He noted it and moved on. There would be time to figure out which one Mason was.

Wrecker said nothing for a long moment. Long enough that Mason started to speak and stopped himself. Then Wrecker held up his left hand, palm out. A scar ran from the base of his index finger across to his wrist — old, healed, flat, the kind that came from something that had taken time to close. "Wrong house," he said. "Wrong family."

He put his hand down. "Kid got hurt." He looked at the camera — not at Avril specifically, but at the screen, at whoever was watching. "I followed orders. Didn't ask questions. Not then." The jaw worked once. "Not anymore." He said it, without sentiment, which made it land harder than if he'd meant it to.

Avril nodded. "Then let's make something worth listening to."

The test came the next morning.

Mason sent a file. Encrypted video, forty seconds. A woman slammed against a warehouse wall, black-bagged, zip-tied. No sound. The timestamp in the corner had been scrubbed, but the metadata hadn't been fully cleaned — Avril found the origin in eleven minutes.

Dr. Lorna Reis. Epidemiologist. Had filed a formal complaint about falsified outbreak data three weeks before the video. Had not been seen since.

He spent four hours building the case file. Cross-referenced the complaint with public health records, traced the facility in the video to a private contractor with federal oversight, and verified Reis's identity through three independent sources. Then he wrote his recommendation: leak to two journalists with track records on national security, protect her identity in the initial coverage, and confirm her status through back channels before anything goes public.

He sent it to the team.

The responses came back within the hour.

Soto: Solid work. Carrick: Good enough. Mason: Told you. Even Wrecker, who communicated almost exclusively in silence, sent back a single thumbs up.

Avril sat with it for a moment — the small, strange satisfaction of having been found adequate by people who didn't give that away cheaply. Then he closed the file and opened the inbox.

It had come in ten days ago—no attachments, no metadata, no way to trace it back.

Just: She never came home. Eliana. Protest. Please.

He'd flagged it when it arrived and then gotten pulled into everything else, and it had sat there in the queue, patient and unanswered. He kept meaning to get to it. He kept not getting to it. That was its own kind of failure, and he knew it.

He read it again now.

She never came home.

Three words that had probably taken someone everything they had to type. A girl. A protest. A door that didn't open again. Somewhere out there, someone was waiting for news that hadn't come, and they'd sent this into the dark because they didn't know where else to send it.

Avril thought about Lina Alvarez calling out her own name as the van doors closed. I see you.

He forwarded it to the team with a single line: I think it's time we found Eliana. He sat with the send confirmation for a moment. Somewhere on the other end of five encrypted relay hops, four people had just received a message from a civilian archivist who had never run an operation, asking them to find a woman they didn't know because someone had sent three words into the dark. It was the most operational thing he'd ever done. He wasn't sure it counted. He understood it didn't matter whether it counted.

Then he sat back and looked at the map on the wall — the pins, the red thread, the crisscrossed lines of a country coming apart at its seams — and felt, for the first time in a long time, like he was exactly where he was supposed to be.

Chapter Four: The Slow Burn

The rain came down soft and insistent on the safehouse roof, the kind that blurred the city into something almost gentle. Avril sat alone in the side room, the others cycling through gear checks and short silences in the next space over. He should have been doing the same. Instead, he was sitting with the past, which had a way of demanding his attention when the future got close enough to touch.

He hadn't slept. Not really. Not in a while. His body obeyed when adrenaline told it to, but his mind ran on a different schedule — drones overhead, data spikes in the comm array, the memory of a feed cutting out at the wrong moment. He could lie still for hours and wake feeling as if something had been working on him in the dark.

He reached into his jacket and found the scarf. Gray wool, faintly scented with cedar and ink. Lena's. He'd had it for three years now, longer than they'd been together, longer than he'd any right to be still carrying it.

She'd believed in small resistance — kindness, community, showing up for your neighbors. When the lists started and the fear set in, she'd wanted to wait it out. He understood that. He'd wanted to want it too. But he couldn't make himself stop looking, and eventually, looking became the only thing he knew how to do, and she needed someone who could also look away.

He'd packed in silence, kissed her forehead, and left without blame. The scarf had been on the hook by the door, and he'd taken it without thinking. Now here he was. He still knew how to reach her. A number he'd never deleted, a Signal address that might or might not still be active. Sometimes he opened the screen and looked at it — not to send anything, but to confirm it was still there, that the thread hadn't gone cold in some way he hadn't been notified about.

He'd done it twice in the past month and then put the phone down without typing. He told himself it was for her safety. If he made contact and they were watching his communications, he'd be drawing a line straight to her. That was true. It was also true that he was afraid of what she might say, or what the silence would mean if she didn't say anything at all. He wasn't sure which of those truths was doing more of the work.

He thought about Trina Cole.

She'd been the reason it crystallized — not the beginning, but the moment he understood what the beginning had been building toward. Sharp-eyed, steady-voiced, the kind of journalist who made people believe the fourth estate was still standing. He'd met her once at a press conference, years before.

She'd bought him coffee, argued with him about press ethics, laughed like someone who still gave a damn. He'd trusted her the way you trust a landmark — not because you've tested it, but because it's always been there.

Then one night he was channel-surfing, and there she was, and her voice was smooth, but her eyes were wrong. Flat. Guarded.

"We remind all citizens that public disruptions, even peaceful ones, can be exploited by bad actors. Stay vigilant. Report any suspicious gatherings. Safety is unity."

He'd seen the same segment two channels later. Different city. Different anchor. Same script.

He found her at the café she used to write in — Java Point, near the university, the same corner table she'd occupied every Thursday morning for the four years he'd known her. He got there first and ordered two coffees. She arrived at 10:03, seven minutes late, which was unlike her. She was wearing sunglasses inside, which was also unlike her. She sat down without being asked and wrapped both hands around the mug he'd ordered for her without looking at it. "You watched the segment," she said. Not a question. "Both of them. Different city, different anchor, same script. Word for word."

She said nothing. Around them, the café did its ordinary business — laptops, conversations, the specific warmth of a room full of people pretending the outside didn't exist. Avril had loved this place once. He'd come here to think, to write. He hadn't been back in months. Being here now felt like visiting a version of himself who'd made different choices. "Didn't sound like you," he said. "No." She turned the mug. "It didn't." "Then why—"

"Because the alternative was losing the platform entirely. Because they don't need to arrest you anymore. They need to dry up the air around you until you can't breathe." Her voice was careful, quiet, the voice she used when reporting something she didn't want to be true. "They've been very good at that. Very patient." He looked at her. She looked at the table. "We all make compromises," she said. "The truth doesn't." Her jaw tightened. "That's easy to say when you're not the one they're watching."

She looked up then, and for a moment the flatness was gone and what was underneath it was something Avril recognized — not fear exactly, but the controlled version of it, the kind you wore when fear had become a permanent weather system, and you'd learned to work in it. "They're watching patterns now. Not just content — intent. The algorithm doesn't wait for you to do something. It decides what you were going to do." "How long have you known?" "Long enough." She looked around the café once, slowly, the sweep of someone checking exits. "Whatever you're building — and I don't want to know what it is, I mean that — stop. Or if you won't stop, make it harder to find. Make it so that by the time they map the pattern, it's already moved."

She reached into her coat pocket and set something on the table between them. A matchbook — black, no logo, one corner torn off cleanly. "If you ever need a back channel. Not this number. Not email. That one." He looked at the matchbook without touching it. "Trina—" "Don't." She stood. "I mean it about not wanting to know. The less I know, the more honest I can be when they ask me." She picked up the mug, took one sip — the first — and set it back down. "For what it's worth, I hope you're careful. And I hope it works. And I hope to God you don't call that number, because if you do, it means something's gone very wrong." She left without finishing the coffee. He sat with the matchbook on the table for a long time before he put it in his pocket. He'd never used it. He still had it.

The Horizon Park protest came a month later. He went to document it — camera and notebook, nothing more. Students, veterans, teachers, the kind of crowd that still believed showing up meant something.

Then the drones came. Three of them, matte-black, silent, the low hum that settled in your stomach before your ears registered it. No warning. Tear gas first, then the tagging. He saw the red dot appear on a man's chest — mid-thirties, Army jacket, holding a sign that read Your Fear Doesn't Equal My Silence. The kinetic round dropped him before he finished reading it.

"Threat subdued," the drone buzzed.

The drone swept back for a second pass, unhurried, running its post-contact assessment. Avril stood there in the open for three full seconds — long enough to be stupid, not long enough to matter — and felt something move through him that wasn't fear and wasn't grief but was the specific, clarifying fury of watching a machine use the word subdued about a man who had been holding a piece of paper. He wanted to throw something. He had nothing to throw. He filed the feeling away in the part of him that was very full of filed feelings and knew it. Avril dragged him behind a refuse bin, pressed a scarf — Lena's scarf, the one he'd thought to grab — to the wound, and lied. You're going to be okay. The footage never aired. The silence wasn't accidental. It was contractual.

He built We Resist that night. Not because he thought it would work. Because he couldn't not.

Soto appeared in the doorway. She read the room in a glance, the way she read everything.

"You good, Greenfellow?"

"Just remembering how we got here."

She considered that. "Don't take too long. Carrick's ready."

The main room had been converted into a command center around a battered folding table covered in printed schematics, hand-annotated in three colors. Carrick stood at the head of it, no uniform, no rank — just the bearing of someone who'd spent twenty years making decisions in bad conditions and hadn't lost the habit.

The new face was Daniels — a former NSA analyst, introduced by Mason as someone who'd burned his clearance getting students out of a surveillance dragnet in Minsk and hadn't looked back. He had the eyes of a man who'd spent a long time staring at data that other people weren't supposed to see. Wrecker sat in the corner, cleaning a component Avril couldn't identify, paying attention to everything.

"Target is a decommissioned telecom relay outside Bellington," Carrick began. "Officially shuttered. What it actually does is run regional crowd surveillance — heat signatures, behavioral flagging, and facial indexing. Everything that keeps a protest from becoming a movement." He tapped the schematic. A squat compound, wooded perimeter, sensor rings marked in red. Not a fortress. Just infrastructure, camouflaged by paperwork.

"Site security is automated," Soto said. "Drones, remote sentry turrets, no onsite personnel. They don't expect anyone to come looking because officially there's nothing to find."

"We're not just disabling it," Carrick continued. "We're pulling everything — logs, footage, command protocols, deployment patterns. We get that data out, and we can prove the regime's been using predictive analytics to suppress dissent before it happens. Before anyone raises a sign. Before anyone makes a call."

"And then we leak it," Avril said.

Daniels nodded once, the kind of nod that meant he'd already thought through exactly how. "Leak it, blast it, embed it. Let people see the playbook. Let them understand they've been living inside a system that was afraid of them before they did anything." He paused. "That's how you break the illusion of safety. Not with outrage. With evidence."

The room settled into quiet. Everyone is looking at the schematic, but nobody is really seeing it.

"We're hitting a federal facility," Carrick said. "On home soil. I want everyone to be clear on what that means before we leave this room."

"The elected government," Soto said. "Or what's left of it."

Avril looked around the table. Ex-soldiers. Former intelligence. People who'd worn the flag and carried out orders in places they weren't allowed to name, and who were now here, in a safehouse in the rain, planning this.

"They may be the government," he said quietly. "But we're the country."

That landed. The room found a new kind of stillness — heavier, but settled.

"We didn't leave the Constitution," Carrick said. "It left us. We're just holding the line." Daniels looked at the table without expression. "I used to get paid to hunt people like us."

"We're not the threat," Soto said. "We're the consequence."

Carrick walked them through the approach. A decoy maintenance van, spoofed utility credentials, Daniels threading their IDs into the access logs in real time. Seven minutes inside the drone sweep window — long enough to reach the command room, pull the surveillance logs, internal comms, flight data, human tagging records, and get out clean. Four encrypted drives, four separate routes, timed dead-drop release to three mirrored dark web repositories. Avril's drive was the priority copy.

"What if they're already watching us?" Avril asked.

Daniels looked at him levelly. "They are." Nobody laughed. Nobody needed to. Carrick placed both hands flat on the table.

"We're not doing this to win a war tonight. We're doing it to remind people that truth still exists. That lies can be exposed. That the machine isn't invincible." He looked at Avril. "Anything to add?"

Avril thought about a man in an Army jacket holding a sign in a park. About Lina Alvarez calling out her own name as the doors closed, about Trina Cole's eyes going flat on a television screen.

"Resistance isn't a crime," he said. "It's an obligation."

Carrick straightened.

"Gear up. Fifteen minutes."

Avril wrapped the scarf around his neck and followed them out.

Chapter Five: Extraction Protocol

The van hit a pothole somewhere north of the sector perimeter, and nobody reacted. That was how Avril knew he was among people who'd done this before — the jolt, the rattle of gear against the walls, the brief lurch of the suspension, and then silence again, everyone exactly where they'd been, breathing the same recycled air.

He'd stopped counting his breaths twenty minutes ago. That felt like progress.

The van's interior was dressed like a utility crew's — tool racks, maintenance stickers, a clipboard on the dash with work orders that didn't match anything real. Beneath it: firepower, encryption, and a hardened data drive in Daniels' coat. Soto sat across from Avril, her plate carrier already adjusted, eyes closed, not sleeping, just conserving. Carrick stood near the front, gripping a ceiling bar, and his stillness reminded Avril of the way certain buildings looked right before a controlled demolition — everything load-bearing, nothing wasted.

Daniels was in the rear corner with a neural deck on his lap, fingers moving in small, precise bursts, scrubbing their transit trail as they rolled — tollgate pings, camera glances, signal handshakes, all of it reshaped or buried in real time. He hadn't looked up since they left the safehouse.

"Ten minutes," Carrick said. "Run it again."

"Target is Eliana Mendez," Soto said, not opening her eyes. "Civil rights attorney. Detained five months ago without charge. No public record of where she's being held. The official story is she disappeared."

"Biometric confirmation?" Carrick asked.

Daniels still didn't look up. "Pulse and retina match at ninety-two percent. She's in there. Still alive. Still sedated."

"Why a relay station?" Avril asked. "Why not a proper detention facility?"

"Compartmentalization," Carrick said. "They use ghost-zoned infrastructure — telecom, utilities, decommissioned grid nodes. No press access, no oversight mandate, no one thinks to file for inspection. It's not a prison. It's just a building that isn't supposed to exist."

Avril looked at Daniels. Something had been sitting in the air since the briefing, unaddressed. "You said you wanted this one specifically. Before we had the full file."

Daniels set the neural deck down on his knee. His face, which normally carried a layer of dry remove between himself and whatever he was doing, was flat in a different way now. Personal.

"My sister was picked up eighteen months ago. Caught on a watchlist for writing letters to a senator — actual letters, paper, nothing encrypted. They held her for eleven days, no charge, no counsel, no call." He paused. "Eliana Mendez took her case pro bono. Pushed until they had to release her or produce a cause. They released her." Another pause, shorter. "Nobody else would touch it."

The van was quiet.

"So that's why," Daniels said, and picked the deck back up.

Carrick gave Avril a look that communicated several things without saying any of them, then turned back to the windshield. "Primary objective is Eliana. Get her out conscious if we can, alive if we can't keep her conscious. Secondary is the data spine — movement patterns, predictive surveillance models, political targeting metrics. Avril, you're with Soto on retrieval. Daniels and I handle the node." He didn't look back. "If you meet resistance, you don't improvise. You get her to the van."

"Understood," Avril said.

Daniels tapped a command and glanced up briefly. "Gate sees a two-person utility crew on repeat inspection. We're clean."

"Let's make history inconvenient," Carrick said, which was apparently something he said, and the van rolled forward.

The facility was aggressively unremarkable. Low concrete, gray, the silhouette of a power substation. A security drone drifted past the outer gate as Carrick and Daniels ran their credentials — a green ping, and it moved on. Avril and Soto followed, pulling a mag sled, and then they were inside, and the door closed behind them, and the city ceased to exist.

"Too clean," Soto said quietly.

She was right. The interior was silent in the specific way of a place that had been recently cleared rather than simply empty. Avril felt it in the back of his neck, the same instinct that had made him good at noticing things in crowds — the absence that was actually a presence.

They split at the junction. Carrick handed Avril a neural beacon synced to Eliana's biosignature. "Medical Sublevel 3. Two floors down. Move."

He and Soto took the stairs.

The beacon pulsed faster as they reached the sublevel. Then it stopped. Avril checked the display. The signal was still active, but the directional arrow had shifted — pointing left toward a sealed door marked INFRASTRUCTURE ACCESS, not right toward the corridor labeled MEDICAL. "Beacon's confused," he said quietly. "Two signal sources. Same biosig."

"Mirror protocol," Soto said, not slowing. "They run a decoy biosignature from a secondary node in case someone's tracking her. Standard in facilities like this." She stopped at the junction and read both corridors. "Medical is right. The beacon wants the echo." "How do you know which is which?" "Because the decoy node doesn't breathe." She moved right without waiting for him to process this. He followed.

He was two seconds behind her — a gap he felt acutely, the particular anxiety of being the least capable in a situation where capability was the whole game. He caught up. He didn't let it happen again. Sterile walls, low light, the faint antiseptic scent of a place designed to keep people alive without letting them be people. Avril had read about facilities like this. He'd documented three of them from the outside. Being inside one felt like stepping into his own archive.

They breached the isolation suite.

Eliana Mendez lay under a thermal blanket, pale, wired to suppression monitors, her breathing shallow but regular. She looked younger than her file photo. She also looked like someone who had been waiting.

Her eyes opened as they came in. For a moment, she looked at Avril without recognition — the eyes of someone whose mind was still finding the surface, processing shape and light before meaning. Her hand moved toward the monitor cable at her wrist in the automatic gesture of someone who had learned to distrust what appeared at her bedside. "Easy," Avril said. "We're not —" "Don't." Her voice was rough, stripped down by weeks of disuse to something harder. "Don't tell me what you are. Tell me who sent you." He hesitated half a beat. "Nobody sent us. We came." She looked at Soto, then back at him. The monitor on her wrist was still reading — he could see it — and it was spiking.

"There was a man," she said slowly. "He came to the door three days ago. Said the same thing. Said they'd come for me." Her jaw tightened. "They hadn't." "We're not him," Avril said. "We're real. And we're on a clock." Something shifted in her expression — not trust, but the decision to operate as though trust were possible. "You're late," she said. "But you came." "We've got you," Avril said. "Can you move?" "In a minute." She blinked, orienting. "They showed me a photograph. Told me someone would come eventually."

She looked at him with the focus of someone fighting sedation, one thought at a time. "They knew your name. And hers." "Whose?" Avril asked, though something in him already knew. But she'd gone under again, her head dropping back against the pillow, whatever clarity she'd summoned already spent.

Soto was already moving, disconnecting monitors with practiced efficiency, working the compression sling under Eliana's shoulders. "She'll be stable for transport. Let's go."

Carrick's voice came over comms just as they reached the stairwell: "Data spine secured. Thirty gigabytes. We're moving — drones activating on sublevel two, guards inbound from the east access." A beat. "Somebody tripped something."

"Working on it," Daniels said, and then there was a burst of static and the sound of something percussive.

They moved through the drainage corridor with Eliana between them, her feet finding the ground in half-steps, Soto's arm across her back. Sirens somewhere above. The shutters on the upper level were sealing — Avril could hear the mechanical sequence, methodical and unhurried, the facility buttoning itself up.

"Forcing a bypass," Carrick said over comms. His voice had gone clipped in the way that meant he was hurt but wasn't going to say so yet. "Be at the gate."

"He's hit," Soto said quietly, not slowing.

"I know."

The gate opened thirty seconds before Avril expected it to. The van was already there, engine running, Daniels at the wheel with blood on his sleeve that wasn't his. Carrick was in the back, hand pressed to his shoulder, directing with his other arm.

They loaded Eliana. Soto pulled the door. Daniels triggered something — a flat crack of displaced air — and behind them, the drones dropped in sequence like lights going out.

The outer gate groaned and opened.

And then they were moving, the facility shrinking in the rear camera, and the city swallowing them the way it always did — without interest, without ceremony, just another vehicle in the dark.

The safehouse was quiet by the time Eliana's vitals stabilized. Carrick's shoulder had been dressed, and he was sitting against the wall with his eyes open, thinking about something he wasn't sharing. Soto stood at the window. Daniels was already working the decrypted files, the data drive open on the table in front of him, thirty gigabytes of the regime's private architecture spreading across his screen.

Avril sat down across from it and started reading.

The files were organized by threat tier — faces, names, time-stamped surveillance logs, and predictive flags. Thousands of people the system had deemed problematic before they'd done anything. He recognized some of the names from the We Resist inbox. He recognized one face from a protest photo he'd archived eight months ago, a man in an Army jacket holding a sign.

He kept scrolling.

And then he stopped.

Her name was in the Tier One watchlist. Flagged and actively monitored. The timestamp on the most recent entry was six days ago.

Lena.

He sat with it for a long time. He was aware, distantly, that his hand had stopped moving. The scrolling had stopped. That he was looking at a name on a screen with the particular stillness of someone who had been braced for something without knowing it and had just felt it arrive. Lena. Tier One. Actively monitored. Six days ago. He made himself read the entry again, the way he read things that mattered — slowly, for accuracy, not for feeling. The flagging criteria: indirect association with documented agitators. Relationship status: former. Contact frequency: none logged in for fourteen months. They had her down as dormant—a connection point to someone dangerous. Not herself, not yet — just adjacent. Just close enough. He thought about the Signal address he'd opened and closed without sending anything. About the number, he hadn't deleted. About how careful he'd been and how irrelevant that carefulness had turned out to be. The room moved around him — Daniels clicking through files, Soto's quiet footsteps, the sound of Eliana breathing steadily from the next room — and he sat there with his hand still on the keyboard and the cursor blinking in the white space below her name, and he did not move for a long time. She'd done everything right. And they'd found her anyway.

Chapter Six: Another Line in the Sand

The safehouse smelled of metal and dried sweat and the particular staleness of a space where people had been making hard decisions for too many hours. Daniels stood at the head of the table with a cracked tablet in his hand and the expression of a man who'd just found something he hadn't wanted to find.

"They took Alex Raines," he said.

Carrick looked up from the field kit he was sorting. "Who's Alex Raines?"

"Analyst. Used to help me sanitize scrape data from transit hubs. Quiet, clean record, doesn't make noise." Daniels tapped the screen. A news crawl bled red across it: U.S. Citizen Deported Under Joint Security Protocol; Held at CECOT. "They picked him up yesterday. Flagged him for a mobility alert near a no-entry corridor in D.C. The official excuse was border violation suspicion under Joint Directive Nine."

"That's not even a law," Avril said.

"Doesn't have to be. They rerouted his identity clearance and ghost-deported him to El Salvador."

Soto said, flatly: "CECOT."

"CECOT," Daniels confirmed.

Carrick set down the field kit. "Absolutely not." "He helped us," Avril said. "He helped us once, which means we owe him gratitude, not a combat op in a foreign country." Carrick's voice was level, final, like certain doors — not locked, just very heavy. "CECOT isn't a domestic relay station. It's a militarized facility in a country that has formally accepted US detainees under a bilateral security agreement our government signed. If we go in there, we're not just breaking laws — we're creating an international incident that hands them every justification they need to label us exactly what they've been calling us." "Which is what?" Avril said. "Insurgents." Carrick looked at him. "Not resistance. Not journalism."

Armed actors operating against state infrastructure across international borders. That's a different matter, legally and practically, and once we're that, we can't become something else again. The room was quiet. Avril could feel the weight of it — not just Carrick's accurate argument, but the fact that Carrick was the one making it. A man who had spent his career inside the machine, saying: Here is where the machine wins. "He's going to disappear," Avril said. "Seventy-two hours."

Carrick was silent for a moment. Then: "I know." He looked at the table. At the schematic. At the clock on the wall. Whatever was happening behind his eyes, he kept it all in. "I know that. And I'm telling you anyway that this is a line we can't uncross." "Then we don't uncross it," Avril said. "We cross it knowing what it costs. Clearly. Out loud. And we carry that."

Carrick looked at him for a long moment. Then he looked at Soto, who said nothing, which was its own answer. He looked at Daniels.

"There's something else," Daniels said. He'd been holding it, Avril could tell. "Alex is scheduled for transfer in seventy-two hours. They're moving him to a non-digital holding block. No telemetry, no signals, no tracks. After that, we won't find him."

The room was quiet.

"Why do you want this one specifically?" Carrick asked Daniels. Not accusatory. Just direct.

Daniels put the tablet down. "Same reason I went after Eliana." He didn't elaborate. Carrick didn't ask him to.

Carrick absorbed that. Then: "We do this my way. The moment planning goes sideways, we abort. Everyone clear?"

Soto nodded. Daniels gave a slow thumbs-up. Avril met Carrick's eyes.

"Let's bring him home," Avril said.

CECOT, Daniels explained, wasn't a prison. It was a prototype — a testbed for predictive containment architecture, every surface mapped, every corridor modeled, every inmate tagged with subdermal telemetry. The main block was segmented into five rings, each isolated. Alex was in Ring Two, standard population with high-value monitoring, which meant they were boxed in from three directions before they'd even started.

Security was mostly automated. Drone-run, AI-flagged. The system analyzed movement, speech, posture — it could mark an anomaly before you acted on it. "The second you sweat wrong, you're tagged," Daniels said.

"That's not surveillance," Soto said. "That's hunting."

"The good news," Daniels continued, pulling up a lower level on the schematic, "is that before this was CECOT, it was a municipal facility. There's a waste channel still registering minimal flow — sludge, not sewage. Leads to an external maintenance port about half a kilometer from the coast."

Carrick raised an eyebrow. "We go in through the pipes."

"Unless you've got a stealth VTOL parked somewhere."

"The tunnel is narrow," Carrick said, sketching on the acetate board. "No cover, no retreat if we're spotted on entry. We need recon, blind zone mapping, and a false signal loop to reach Ring Two. And we need someone who knows the terrain." He looked at Soto.

"There's a man," she said. "Worked on engineering contracts at the facility before the conversion. Goes by Camaleón. He's not trustworthy — but he hates uniforms more than he likes money."

"We don't need to trust him," Carrick said. "We need him to hate the right people."

Daniels looked up. "We're also on a clock. Sixty hours to transfer."

Carrick drew a circle over the entire diagram with a red pen. "Then we go in sixty. Make contact today. If he's in, we roll prep immediately."

The port district of San Miguel smelled of brine and fried oil and the particular exhaustion of a place that had been working too hard for too long. The sun was dropping behind the rooftops when Avril and Soto pushed through the door of a seafood shack that had no name on the outside and a jukebox on the inside playing something tinny and half-remembered.

The man in the back booth had a weather-beaten face, mirrored sunglasses, and a ceramic mug of rum he was working through without urgency. He didn't look up when they came in.

Soto placed a folded slip of thermal paper on the table. It bore the image of a uniform patch from the facility's original build phase. A credential that meant nothing now except as a signal — I know what this was before it became what it is.

Camaleón took a sip of rum. "What you want is expensive," he said, without moving. "What you need is suicidal."

"And yet here we are," Soto said.

He looked at them for the first time. "CECOT has ghosts in its tunnels. You make noise in the wrong one, they don't send guards." He tapped the rim of his mug. "They seal it behind you and let the systems work."

Avril sat down across from him. "Then help us avoid the noise."

Camaleón laughed, a short, quiet sound. "Americans. Always think that if you plan hard enough, you can cheat death." He looked at his mug for a moment, then back at them. "There's a maintenance panel under the seawall. Rusted shut — no one's touched it since before the upgrade. I can show you where it is. After that, you're on your own."

"That'll do," Avril said.

Camaleón stood. "Tomorrow. Four in the morning. Bring gear that doesn't cry when it gets wet." He paused at the door and looked back, not unkindly. "You're not the first to try something stupid at CECOT. Just make sure you're the first not to die doing it."

He walked out into the dark.

Soto watched the door close. "He's in."

"Then so are we," Avril said.

The night before an op had its own texture. Gear was laid out and reassembled, then laid out again. Conversations that were shorter than they needed to be and silences that were longer. Avril sat with Carrick in the back corridor for an hour while Carrick walked him through close-quarters movement in confined spaces — stance narrow, weight forward, no sudden pivots. He hit the padded wall three times before he stopped telegraphing. Carrick didn't comment on the improvement, which was how Avril knew there had been one.

He thought about Lena's name in the watchlist. He'd been thinking about it in the gaps between everything else, the way you think about a thing you haven't decided what to do with yet. She'd done everything right. She'd tried to stay invisible. It hadn't worked. He didn't know if she knew. He didn't know how to warn her without putting her in more danger. He folded the scarf tighter inside his jacket and put it away.

Not now. After.

An hour before they were due to leave, Carrick found Avril in the corridor and stood there for a moment without speaking. Then: "I want to say something before we go in." "Okay," Avril said. "The op is solid. The plan is as good as it gets with the resources and time we have." He paused. "That doesn't mean we come back. Any of us. I've done enough of these to know that solid and clean aren't the same thing, and I don't want anyone walking into those pipes thinking this is low-risk just because we planned it carefully." Avril said nothing. "I'm not trying to talk you out of it," Carrick said. "I already tried that."

"I'm just saying — if you have something to do before we go, someone to reach, or something you've been putting off — now is when you do it." He held Avril's gaze. "Not after." He went back to prepping his kit. Avril stood in the corridor for a moment. He thought about the number he hadn't deleted. The Signal address.

The thing he'd been putting off. He took out the scarf and held it for a moment. Then he put it back, shouldered his bag, and went to join the others. Camaleón was waiting at the seawall when they arrived, hunched in a battered windbreaker, chewing the end of an unlit cigar. He kicked aside a drift of seaweed to reveal a half-buried service hatch sealed under layers of corroded mesh and a reinforced bolt plate.

"Feeds into the overflow tunnel under Ring Three," he said. "Stinks like death. But it's dry. Mostly."

Soto dropped to one knee and applied cutting solvent to the old metal, watching the oxidation hiss away. Above them, the sky was moonless, clouds rolling heavy, the kind of cover you couldn't plan for and were grateful when it arrived.

"Forty minutes before the thermal sensors wake up," Camaleón said. He accepted a sealed envelope from Daniels without looking at it and tucked it into his coat. "You want me to wish you luck?"

"We want you to disappear," Carrick said.

Camaleón gave a lazy salute and walked into the dark.

The hatch came free with a shriek of metal. Cold black air rushed out. Carrick clicked on his red-beam torch.

"Stack up."

The tunnel swallowed them. Ankle-deep runoff, rusted pipes overhead, every breath tasting of mildew and decay. Avril moved second in line behind Carrick, headlamp dimmed to red, tracking the silhouette ahead. Soto marked each intersection with a chalk sigil. Daniels counted seconds in a murmur from the rear.

Carrick halted—closed fist.

A vibration moved through the walls — mechanical, rhythmic, not yet close. Patrol sweep. He gestured forward: slow advance.

They reached the substation bulkhead. Soto attached a thermal strip and sliced the bolts. Steam hissed, the smell of coolant bleeding through the seal.

"Behind here is Ring Two's environmental corridor," she whispered. "No shadows, no dead zones. We move fast."

The hatch opened. Red light spilled in. They slipped through.

The corridor was low and smooth, surveillance markers blinking from the ceiling seams like mechanical fireflies. Daniels knelt at a wall panel and slotted a slim rod into the maintenance interface. The lights dimmed one step further.

"Protocol mask injected. Seven minutes."

They moved through the passage. Through clear panes above, Avril could make out the shapes of drones sliding along ceiling rails. He kept his breathing shallow and even and thought about nothing except the next corner.

A reinforced door: 2B-Sec13. Daniels flashed the biometric reader.

MATCH: ALEX RAINES.

Carrick tapped Avril's shoulder. "You open. We cover."

Avril keyed the sequence. The lock hissed green. The door slid open.

Alex Raines sat against the wall. Pale, unshaven, eyes wide with the specific disbelief of someone who has stopped expecting anything good. He looked at them and didn't move.

"Jesus," he said. "They actually came."

After a moment, he said, "Prove it. Say something only Daniels would know."

Daniels stepped forward and crouched low. "You had a cat. Your landlord tried to evict you for it. You blackmailed him with a heat sensor map from his illegal crypto rig upstairs."

Alex let out a long breath. "Okay. You're real." He pushed himself up slowly, knees unsteady. "They kept telling me you were coming, then telling me you weren't. Every few days. I stopped believing either."

"Believe it now," Soto said from the door. "We move."

Avril offered his hand, and Alex took it, his grip shaking. "You do know there's no way out of here, right?"

"There is now," Carrick said and stepped into the corridor.

They made it three corridors before Daniels' timer hit yellow. Then an alarm chirped — two notes, quiet, out of rhythm — and Daniels said "grid's rebooting," and Carrick said "pick it up," and the pace shifted from controlled to urgent without anyone deciding to run.

Alex stumbled once. Avril caught him, kept him upright. "You're not dying in a pipe," he said, which wasn't reassuring exactly but was something to hold onto.

They reached the bulkhead. Soto triggered the thermal override — steam, louder than before, too loud — and overhead, a ceiling drone paused mid-glide.

"They see us," Soto said.

Daniels threw a microflare down the corridor, IR static flooding the sensors. The drone hesitated. The hatch swung open. They piled through — Alex first, then Avril, then Carrick, then Daniels. Soto came last, firing a suppressive round into the drone's optics before she slipped through and slammed the hatch behind her.

Red light surged on the other side.

They ran. The tunnel strobed behind them as the lockdown engaged, feet splashing through runoff, the alarm now a full roar above. A pulse round spat out of the dark and sparked off the wall near Avril's shoulder. Soto spun and returned fire. A drone crashed into the grim. Another accelerated — Carrick dropped to one knee, three-round burst, center mass, and it slammed into the wall.

"Port seal," Daniels called. "Twenty meters."

He hit the hatch release. They tumbled out into salt air and breaking waves and a sky just starting to gray at the edges. Carrick came through last and sealed the hatch behind him.

Above, on the cliffs, spotlights snapped on.

Carrick keyed his throat mic. "Camaleón. Window's closed. Where's our ride?"

Static. Then: "Two minutes. North Beach."

They moved low along the craggy shore, weaving between boulders as searchlight beams swept the rock above them. Soto half-carried Alex up the incline without slowing. A drone's rotor grew louder overhead, and Carrick hurled a beacon flare into the rocks behind them — a burst of infrared heat that blinded sensors for a moment, long enough.

A skimmer boat materialized in the fog offshore, camouflaged under mesh netting, running silent.

Soto shoved Alex aboard. Daniels pulled Avril in behind. Carrick took one last look at the bluff — searchlights sweeping the place they'd just been — and jumped.

The boat peeled away. The alarms faded behind them into the sound of the sea.

By the time they reached the safehouse, Alex's hands had mostly stopped shaking. He sat in a corner wrapped in a thermal blanket, sipping weak coffee, while Daniels sat nearby without crowding him, which was its own kind of language. For the first twenty minutes, he said nothing. He sipped the coffee in small sips and stared at the wall with the focused attention of someone whose mind was working through a backlog — cataloguing what had happened, comparing it against expectations, locating himself in time and space.

Avril had seen it before, in people who had been inside a system designed to make them stop expecting anything good. Coming out the other side required recalibration. You couldn't rush it. Then, quietly, Alex said, "I thought you weren't real." Daniels looked at him. "The last two weeks. Every few days, they'd tell me someone was coming. Then they'd tell me you weren't. Back and forth." He turned the mug in his hands. "I stopped believing either. And then I started wondering if the whole thing — you, We Resist, any of it — was something they'd made up. Part of the system. To see what I'd do."

He looked at Daniels. "I wasn't sure until you said the thing about the cat," Daniels said nothing. He didn't need to. "I want you to know," Alex said, "that I didn't give them anything. I know what that sounds like. I know it's what anyone would say. But I need to say it anyway." "We know," Avril said. Alex looked at him. Something crossed his face — not quite relief, not quite recognition. Something more complicated than either. "Okay," he said. "Okay." He didn't say anything else for a while. Neither did anyone else. The safehouse made its quiet sounds around them.

Carrick stood at the head of the room. He looked tired in a specific way — the wound in his shoulder from the Bellington op still pulling, the new hours stacked on top of the old ones — but his eyes were clear.

"You held out longer than most would've," he said to Alex.

Alex looked up. "You got me out. That's more than anyone else even tried."

Avril leaned forward. "They told you someone was coming. What else did they show you?"

Alex was quiet for a moment. "Your site. Photographs. Names. Some were flagged, some were called tested. They knew more than they should've." He looked at Avril. "They knew about you specifically. They were watching you before We Resist launched. They wanted me to confirm details."

"Did you?" Carrick asked.

"No." A beat. "They didn't believe me."

Avril sat back. He thought about Eliana's half-conscious words — they knew your name, and hers — and about Lena's name in the watchlist, and about the way the machine had apparently been watching all of them for longer than any of them had known. Not reacting. Preparing.

"This wasn't just a proof of concept for the surveillance system," Carrick said. "Alex was bait. They wanted to see if we'd come."

The room absorbed that.

"And now they know we will," Soto said.

Avril looked at the decrypted files still open on the table — thousands of names, faces, timestamps, the regime's private map of everyone it considered a problem. Somewhere in there was Lena. Somewhere in there, probably, were people who didn't even know they were being watched.

He thought about what it meant that the machine had been patient enough to wait.

And then he thought about what it meant that they'd come anyway.

Chapter Seven: Regroup

The National Security Advisor had the kind of stillness that meant she was angrier than she was showing.

"So." She tapped her pen against the folder. "Someone extracted a detainee from an allied facility using black-market tunnel access and compromised military-grade technology. Clean. No bodies, no signature, no trace."

The analyst across the table nodded carefully.

"And you're confident it was them."

"The profiles line up. We believe Avril Greenfellow was directly involved."

She leaned back. Outside her window, Washington moved through its ordinary business — motorcades, press briefings, the machinery of governance running on schedule. She looked at it for a moment before she spoke again.

"They're getting better," she said. It wasn't a compliment. It was a problem statement.

"Yes, ma'am."

"Find out who's resourcing them. Find out who knew this was coming. And find out—" she closed the folder — "how a civilian archivist ends up running extraction ops on allied soil without anyone seeing it coming until it was over."

She dismissed him with a look.

In San Salvador, the Minister of Internal Surveillance was less composed.

"Our systems were penetrated by volunteers," he said, and the word came out like something he'd bitten. "No nation-state affiliation. No military backing, we can confirm. People with conviction and a grudge." He slammed the tablet onto the table. "That makes us look like amateurs."

A figure at the far end of the table spoke without looking up. "Not just vulnerable. Exposed. The question is whether we respond visibly or quietly."

"Quietly," the Minister said. "Increase the suppression sweeps. And I want to know who in the private sector had advance knowledge of this operation." A pause. "If they come again—"

"If they come again," the figure said, still calm, "we erase the facility. No prisoner, no proof, no story."

The room absorbed that without objection.

Three time zones away, in a safehouse that smelled of iodine and cold coffee, nobody felt like they'd won anything.

Alex Raines sat on the edge of a metal cot with a blanket around his shoulders, his eyes moving from face to face with the particular alertness of someone who had recently learned that stillness was dangerous. He'd said very little since the debrief.

Avril didn't push him. Some things needed time before they became words.

Eliana was awake. She'd come back to herself gradually over the previous day — not all at once, but in increments, the sedation lifting in stages. She sat at the table now with both hands wrapped around a mug, and though she was pale and moved carefully, her eyes were clear. When she looked at Avril, she held the look long enough to let him know she remembered what she'd said before losing consciousness. She didn't repeat it. Neither did he. Not yet.

Reyes stood by the window. He was new to this particular safehouse — a logistics coordinator who'd been working the Sanctuary concept in the background for weeks, sourcing properties and building identity infrastructure through shell companies in jurisdictions with low scrutiny. Soto had brought him in quietly. He was compact, pragmatic, constitutionally skeptical, and he had the manner of someone who had spent a long time making problems disappear and had few illusions about the cost of it.

"He can't stay here," Reyes said, nodding toward Alex.

"We know," Avril said. "That's what we're solving."

The Sanctuary idea had been forming for weeks — longer, if Avril was honest, since the night he first built We Resist and understood that exposure without protection was just a different kind of abandonment. You couldn't pull people out of black sites and then leave them to find their own way. You needed somewhere for them to go.

Reyes had been working on the infrastructure end. Shell companies, layered corporate ownership, properties in stable low-scrutiny countries — remote towns, island outskirts, the edges of sprawling cities where a quiet household attracted no particular attention. He spread a working map across the table and walked them through what existed so far: three properties at various stages of readiness, two identities per site operator, communication links that didn't touch any of their existing channels.

"The gaps are staffing and funding," he said. "We need people who know how to move others quietly across borders. Ex-consular staff, travel advisors, people who understand surveillance infrastructure well enough to route around it. And we need them to be untraceable back to us."

"The benefactors will fund it," Eliana said. "If we frame it right. This isn't a luxury — it's what makes everything else sustainable. You can't keep asking people to risk everything if there's nowhere to land."

Alex had been listening without speaking. Now he said, quietly: "Just don't let them find me again." He wasn't asking for a promise. He was stating the requirement.

"That's what we're building," Avril said.

Alex had been quiet through the Sanctuary discussion, which Avril had taken as exhaustion. He understood now, watching him, that it was something else. Alex was listening — carefully, with the particular attention of someone cataloguing exits. When there was a pause, he said: "How do I know this place doesn't already have a file on me?" The room stilled. Not defensively — it was a fair question. "You don't," Avril said. "Not yet. That's the honest answer. We're asking you to extend trust on the basis of the fact that we came when we said we would." Alex looked at him for a moment. "That's a thin basis." "It's the only one we've got right now," Avril said. "We're building the rest." Alex nodded slowly — the nod of someone who understood the terms and had decided, provisionally, to accept them. "Okay," he said. "But I'm watching." He said it without hostility. Just information. "Good," Avril said. "So are we." It was Eliana who lit the match, which Avril suspected she'd been holding since she woke up.

"Are we doing this again?" she asked. Not hostile — careful. "Black site extractions. Military ops. Is that what we are now?"

"We had actionable intel and a closing window," Reyes said. "We moved. It worked."

"I know it worked. I was there — unconscious, but there." She set her mug down. "That's not what I'm asking. I'm asking what we become if this is the pattern. Because We Resist started as a signal. A light that people could see. If we turn into something else, we lose that. And I don't think we get it back."

Reyes looked like he wanted to argue. Carrick, from the corner where he'd been quiet since sitting down, said nothing, which Avril had learned meant he was listening harder than usual.

"She's right that it's a question," Avril said. "She's also right that it doesn't have a clean answer." He looked at Alex. "When a government disappears its own citizens, and there's no one left to speak for them, we become their voice. Sometimes that's a broadcast. Sometimes — when the window is sixty hours and closing — it's something else." He paused. "We don't make it the norm. But we don't pretend we didn't do it, either. And we don't pretend the next Alex won't come."

Eliana was quiet for a moment. "Then Sanctuary isn't optional. It's what makes the rest of this defensible. If we're going to pull people out, we have to have somewhere to put them."

"Agreed," Carrick said. First word he'd spoken in twenty minutes. It landed accordingly.

Reyes sat back, jaw tight but settled. The argument wasn't over — it would keep surfacing, as it should — but for now it had found its resting place.

Mason had been running the applicant queue while the team was in the field. He'd flagged one.

"Jordan Myers," he said, pulling up the file. "Cryptographic engineer. Worked on secure mesh networks. Been reaching out for three weeks — we finally cleared him for a virtual meet." He paused. "He has a Carnegie Mellon degree, three years at a private cybersecurity firm in Denver, then a move to open-source privacy tools under the alias TraceZero. Clean record, minimal social footprint, Reddit history consistent with passive activist engagement." Another pause, longer. "It's very clean."

"Too clean?" Avril asked.

"That's what I wanted you to see for yourself."

Jordan appeared on screen twenty minutes later: early thirties, composed, the particular articulateness of someone who had prepared carefully without wanting to look like he had. His ideas were good — a low-latency decentralized chat application bouncing through volunteer nodes worldwide, genuinely innovative in its approach to state-level surveillance resistance. He knew his material. He said the right things.

He also asked where they were based. Who made the final decisions? Whether there was a real command structure beneath the distributed appearance.

Avril deflected each one without making it look like a deflection, which was its own kind of exhausting. After the call ended, he sat for a moment looking at the blank screen.

"He's good," Mason said.

"Yes," Avril said. "That's the problem." Wrecker had been in the doorway for most of the call. He hadn't said anything during it, which wasn't unusual. He spoke now. "He blinked wrong." Mason looked up. "What?" "When you asked him about his last employer. He answered the question, but his eyes went left first. Half a second. You learn to clock that." Wrecker shrugged, the particular shrug of someone who had spent years in rooms where reading bodies was the difference between operational and not. "Could be nothing. A lying reflex from a job he doesn't want to talk about. Could be he's running a different script than the one he's showing you." He pushed off the doorframe. "Just saying. The tech is real. Doesn't mean the person is." He went to bed. Avril sat with that for a while.

Later, when most of the safehouse had gone quiet, Eliana found Avril at the table with Jordan's encrypted message threads open on the laptop. She sat down across from him without being invited, which he'd come to understand was how she operated.

"He asked for too much, too fast," she said. "Or he's exactly who he says he is and he's overeager," Avril said. "We've burned people before for fitting too well." "I know." She looked at the screen. "What bothers me isn't whether he's a plant. It's the timing. We come back from two operations, the government knows our network better than we thought, Alex tells us they've had a file on you since before launch — and now a very clean, very capable applicant appears and starts asking structural questions." Avril said nothing. "What if he's a distraction?" Eliana said. "What if we spend the next two weeks running Jordan Myers to ground and the actual problem is somewhere we're not looking?" She paused. Then: "Can I say something else?" "Yes." "You started this because you couldn't look away.

That was the thing; you were the person who couldn't stop watching, couldn't stop documenting, couldn't stop making the record. That's what We Resist is. It's you refusing to look away." She looked at him directly. "But you've been looking inward for weeks now. At the team. At who might be wrong. At Jordan Myers' blinking pattern. And I'm watching you become someone so focused on the threat inside the room that you've stopped watching what's happening outside it." She stood. "That's not a criticism. It's a question. Are you still the person who started this? Or are you becoming someone else?" Avril said nothing. "You think someone's already inside," Avril said.

She didn't answer. She didn't have to. She just held his gaze long enough to make sure he understood she wasn't speculating.

Then she got up and went to bed.

Avril stayed at the table. The cursor blinked in Jordan's message thread. Outside, the city made its indifferent sounds. He thought about how long the machine had been watching before any of them knew to look back.

He thought about Lena's name in the watchlist.

He thought about a matchbook with one corner torn off, sitting in his jacket pocket, unused.

He didn't sleep.

Chapter Eight: Lines of Trust

The wind coming off the Atlantic arrived in gusts, rattling the shutters of the hillside property just outside Porto. Reyes stood at the edge of the gravel path and scanned the structure with the practiced stillness of someone who had once been paid to anticipate worst-case scenarios rather than avoid them.

"Feels exposed," he said.

Eliana stopped beside him, hands in her coat pockets. "Everything feels exposed if you look at it long enough."

"That's not pessimism." He turned toward the back of the property, checking sightlines. "That's operational memory."

The woman who owned the place was in her sixties, wiry and sun-leathered, with the particular economy of movement that came from decades of watching people arrive and leave without asking why. She offered them coffee, but they declined. She shrugged and led them through the back door and down to the boat dock, where the water was gray-green, and the nearest neighbor was three hundred meters away through pine.

"People come through sometimes," she said, in accented English that suggested she'd had this conversation before. "Artists. Families. Dissidents, once or twice. No one stays long."

"Would you be comfortable not knowing why they're here?" Eliana asked.

"I'm comfortable with the money clearing and the questions stopping." She said it without edge — a statement of terms, not hostility. "That's the rule."

Reyes circled the dock, noting the access point, the low profile from the road above. Quiet. Private. The kind of place that looked like nothing from a distance, which was exactly what it needed to look like.

On the drive back, he said, "We run it through one of the shell companies. Utilities under aliases. Communication links off the existing grid entirely."

Eliana watched the coastline pass. "Node One," she said.

"Just one of many," Reyes replied. "Assuming we build fast enough."

He didn't say: faster than they're moving against us. He didn't need to.

The message from Grey Sentinel arrived at 4:17 a.m., routed through three relays and a dead drop that hadn't been used in six weeks. Avril found it when he woke at five, still in the same clothes he'd fallen asleep in, still at the table where Eliana had left him.

The message was eight words: I have names. I need to look you in the eye.

He read it twice. Then he closed the laptop and sat in the dark for a while, listening to the building settle.

Grey Sentinel had been a thread for weeks — Tier 4 clearance, claims of files, names, and locations from inside the apparatus, and requests for in-person contact on neutral ground. The intelligence was too specific to dismiss and too unverified to act on. Every time a meeting was proposed, something intervened: the Bellington op, the CECOT extraction, the aftermath. The thread had stayed open and unpulled, accumulating weight.

I have names.

Avril didn't ask himself whether it was a trap. He already knew it might be. The question was whether the cost of not going exceeded the cost of going, and by how much.

By seven, he had made his decision. By eight, he had a location — a reading room in the back of an antiquarian bookshop in Lisbon, ninety minutes away. Neutral enough. Public enough. Small enough that someone running surveillance would have to get close.

He told Carrick. Nobody else.

The bookshop smelled of old paper and lemon oil and the particular silence of a room that had absorbed a hundred years of people pretending to read while they watched the door. Avril arrived twenty minutes early and spent them with a water-stained atlas open on his knees, seeing none of it.

Grey Sentinel arrived at the exact agreed time, which told Avril something. He was younger than the clearance level suggested — early forties, compact, with the careful posture of someone who had spent years learning how to look unremarkable. He sat down across from Avril and placed nothing on the table between them.

"You're the archivist," he said.

"You have names," Avril said.

A beat. The man looked at the atlas, then at Avril's hands, then at his face. Whatever he was checking for, he seemed to find it.

"Three names inside your network," he said. "Not suspected — confirmed. One has been passing location metadata through a deprecated channel for four months. One provided the pattern analysis that made the Bellington intercept possible." He paused. "One you haven't questioned yet because you trust them."

Avril kept his face still. "And you have this how?"

"Because they came to us first." He said it quietly, without apology. "Or someone like us. The offer was declined. The names were logged. The file exists, and I'm the one who has it, and if you want it, you'll need to decide whether you trust me enough to take the meeting that comes after this one."

"What meeting?"

"A principal's meeting. Neutral site, three days out. You, your operational lead, and two people from my side who are not on the side you think they're on." He folded his hands. "I know how that sounds. I also know you've been sitting on a file of your own for a while now. And I know the name at the top of it isn't the name you need to be worried about."

The lemon oil. The old paper. Somewhere in the shop, a door opened and closed.

Avril said, "How do I verify you're not one of them?"

"You don't," Grey Sentinel said. "Not today. That's the condition of the meeting. You come knowing it might be a trap and you come anyway, because the alternative is staying blind, and you've been blind long enough."

He stood. Left nothing behind. Walked out past the shelves without hurrying and, in thirty seconds, was gone into the Lisbon morning as though he'd never been there.

Avril sat for another five minutes. The atlas was still open on his knees. He looked at it now — a spread of coastlines from the 1960s, boundaries that had since been redrawn. He thought about how much the map had looked like the truth and how much it had simply been the best available approximation at the time.

He closed it and went outside to where Carrick was waiting.

"Well?" Carrick said.

"I need you to clear three days," Avril said. "And I need you to tell me everything you know about our Tier One vulnerabilities. Not what's in the report. What you actually know."

Carrick looked at him for a long moment. "You're going."

"I'm going."

Something shifted in Carrick's jaw — not quite resignation, not quite approval. "Then I'm going with you."

Back at the safehouse, Mason had made progress on Jordan Myers. Not progress toward a verdict — progress toward a sharper version of the question.

He'd run the technical evaluation in stages: access to a sandboxed environment, a communications test on a non-operational relay, a piece of documentation with a subtle inconsistency buried four layers deep. Jordan had caught the inconsistency within two hours. He'd flagged it through exactly the right channel. He'd noted that someone had seeded test bait in the back layer and asked, mildly, whether that was intentional.

"Good catch," Eliana had told him when she ran the test.

"Was it a test?" he'd asked.

"Everything is," she'd said, and watched his face.

He'd nodded slowly, like someone who had expected exactly that answer and still wasn't sure how to feel about it. It was the most human response he'd given in three days of evaluation — not the smoothness, not the technical fluency, but that nod—the small collapse of composure into something that looked like actual consideration.

Avril reviewed the session logs that evening. Smart, he thought. Careful. Both. But neither answer closed the question. The problem with someone genuinely skilled was that their performance of trustworthiness looked identical to the real thing, right up until the moment it didn't.

He left Jordan's file open and moved to the other one.

The folder was labeled PERSISTENT/RED, tucked behind three authentication layers that Avril had added incrementally over the months, each one placed during a moment of doubt so specific he could date them.

He had started the file the week after the logistics drop in Spain — a routine courier run, intercepted with a precision that required foreknowledge. The official explanation had been a tracking device, left by accident in an outbound crate. Avril had accepted it because he needed to, and then he'd opened a new folder and begun writing down the things that didn't feel right.

Time delays in responses that should have been immediate. A ping to a deprecated server from a device that had no operational reason to know that server's address. A briefing that had been summarized, in conversation two days later, with a detail that hadn't been in the written record — a detail that could only have come from someone present.

None of it was enough. That was the thing about the file. None of it had ever been enough to bring to anyone, because the act of bringing it would require him to name a direction of suspicion, and he didn't know yet whose direction to name. So he kept writing things down, and the file kept growing. The entries had names beside them — not accusations, just notations. A date, a room, an anomaly, a name. Carrick, three times: once for the Spain logistics drop, twice for timing that could be explained by the shoulder wound and the extra hours it was costing him.

Mason, twice: once for the deprecated server ping, once for a briefing summary that had circulated with a detail that shouldn't have been included. Reyes, once, and he'd almost removed it — the entry was thin, a delay with a reasonable explanation he hadn't fully verified. None of them added up. That was the thing. Any one of them, taken alone, was noise. Together, they were still probably noise. But the file existed because noise sometimes resolved into signal, and the only way to know which was which was to keep the record. He looked at the name at the top of the folder. Not Carrick. Not Mason. Not Reyes.

Someone older than all of them in the network, someone whose presence he'd come to rely on the way you relied on a piece of infrastructure — without examining it, because examining the things you relied on made them fragile. That was exactly the problem. And every time he looked someone in the eye during a briefing, he was aware of the quiet weight of it, sitting behind the authentication layers, patient as a debt.

Grey Sentinel had said: the name at the top of it isn't the name you need to be worried about.

Which meant he had the file too. Or knew what was in it—or both.

Avril stared at the name at the top of the folder for a long time. Someone trusted. Someone who had been here before he'd understood what he was building — who had, in fact, been in the room the night he first understood what he was building. A night six months ago, when the inbox had hit ten thousand messages, and he'd sat at the table not knowing whether to feel something had begun or something had gone too far, and this person had sat across from him and said, "You built something real."

Not a compliment. A statement of fact delivered in a register that made it feel like a warning. He'd trusted them more after that. He trusted careful people. He trusted people who understood the weight of things. He thought about all the times that person had been in the room when things went wrong, and all the times they hadn't been. The problem was that the pattern could be read both ways — as evidence of betrayal or as the noise of shared risk. He'd been reading it both ways for months. He didn't know how to stop.

He didn't sleep. He sat at the table with the folder open, the window dark, and the building settling around him. He thought about Lena's name on the watchlist, the matchbook still in his jacket pocket with one corner torn off, and the principals meeting in three days, which might be the most important thing they'd ever do or the last. Outside, the city made its indifferent sounds. He thought about how the machine had been watching before any of them knew to look back. He thought about how long patience could be mistaken for loyalty. He closed the folder. He opened a new document — blank, no filename, behind the same three authentication layers. He typed one word at the top: SHADOW. Then he sat back and thought about what he was going to put under it. He didn't sleep. But when morning came, the document had four entries.

Chapter Nine: Neutral Ground

The NSA Advisor received the intercept at six in the morning, before her coffee, which meant she read it twice, standing at her desk in the gray light, before she allowed herself to sit down.

The routing was clean — too clean, in the way that things scrubbed by someone who knew exactly what traces to remove still left the outline of their absence. What remained was a fragment: a meeting request, relayed through a dead channel that her office had flagged as dormant, from a source her counterintelligence division had been building a profile on for eleven months. A source they had never been able to place.

She read the fragment a third time. Then she called the one person in the building whose opinion she trusted more than her own on questions of this particular kind.

"Grey Sentinel made contact," she said when he picked up.

A pause. "With them."

"With them."

Another pause, longer. "That's either the most useful thing that's happened in six months," he said, "or the most dangerous."

"I know," she said. "Find out which."

She hung up and looked out at the city waking below her. She thought about a civilian archivist sitting somewhere in Europe, reading a message that had cost a great deal to deliver, deciding whether to trust it. She thought about how much she would give to be in the room when he decided.

She thought: they're getting better. And still the problem statement, not a compliment.

The meeting site was a municipal archive outside Geneva — Carrick's choice, which Avril had accepted without argument. Three floors of climate-controlled document storage, public-facing reading rooms on the ground level, and a parking structure with four exits. Carrick had walked it twice in the preceding days while Avril stayed off the street. He'd identified two positions from which the room could be surveilled and confirmed both were empty. That left the positions he couldn't identify, which was the part neither of them mentioned aloud.

They arrived separately. Avril first, through the main entrance, with a reader's card in a name that had existed for four years and had never done anything suspicious. He found a table in the reading room and opened a bound volume of municipal land records from 1962 and waited.

Carrick came in through a side entrance eight minutes later and took a position near the door without sitting down. He had the particular quality of stillness that large men sometimes develop — not passive, but compressed—a held thing. Avril had learned to read Carrick's stillness the way you read weather: the degree of compression told you something about what he'd assessed. Right now, the compression is high. Not alarm — readiness. The difference mattered. Twice during the meeting, Carrick shifted his weight slightly, almost imperceptibly, to his right — a movement Avril had come to understand meant someone had moved closer behind him. Both times, Avril kept his eyes on Grey Sentinel and did not turn around. Both times, after a moment, the weight shifted back. Whatever Carrick had seen had resolved or moved on. The third time he shifted, he didn't shift back.

Grey Sentinel's two people arrived together, which Avril noted. A woman, late fifties, with the careful posture of someone who had once been very important and had learned to carry it quietly. A man, younger, who scanned the room once on entry in a way that was either a professional habit or a tell, and who then didn't scan it again, which suggested the former.

Grey Sentinel himself came in two minutes after them, from the main entrance, alone. Avril had been in the reading room for twenty minutes before the others arrived. He'd spent them with a water-stained atlas open on his knees, seeing none of it, watching the room instead. Eleven people had passed through in that time. He'd noted the exits, the sightlines, the positions of the staff. He'd registered the man at the far table who had arrived before him — a heavy volume open, turning a page at intervals that felt slightly too regular—not reading speed. Something else. He filed it. Either it was nothing, or it was something they couldn't act on in this room. The meeting proceeded either way.

He sat down across from Avril the same way he had in the Lisbon bookshop — nothing on the table, weight settled, unhurried like someone who had made a decision a long time ago and was executing it now.

"You came," he said.

"You knew I would," Avril said.

"I hoped." He glanced once at Carrick, acknowledged him with a minimal nod that Carrick did not return. "I want to introduce the people I brought. Not their names — not yet. But their relevance."

The woman spoke first. Her English carried the trace of something mid-European, worn smooth by years of use. She had worked, she said, in treaty compliance verification for eleven years before the administration she'd served under was replaced by one that found treaty compliance inconvenient. She had files. Not copies — originals, with provenance chains that would hold up to forensic review. Procurement records showing the routing of domestic surveillance infrastructure through defense contractor subsidiaries. The kind of documentation that didn't prove wrongdoing so much as it made wrongdoing undeniable.

The younger man had worked cyber operations for a three-letter agency whose name he didn't say and didn't need to.

He'd burned his clearance quietly, which meant he still had friends who hadn't. He knew, he said, how the targeting architecture worked from the inside. He knew which nodes were active and which were legacy cover. He knew how to tell the difference between a surveillance trace and a ghost — a file maintained to look current while its subject had already been quietly reclassified.

"Reclassified how?" Avril said.

The man looked at him steadily. "Moved from monitor to action."

The room was very quiet for a moment. Somewhere above them, a ventilator ticked in the ductwork.

"The name at the top of your file," Grey Sentinel said. "I told you it wasn't the one you needed to worry about. I can tell you now why." He paused. "Because that person was moved to action status eight weeks ago. Not for what they've done. For what they know. The threat isn't from inside your network. The threat is that someone outside it has decided that person is a liability."

Avril kept his face still. He thought about the name he'd been sitting with for months, the one he'd been watching with the particular anguish of someone who suspects the worst and can't prove it. He thought about how different those two things were — betrayal and exposure — and how much they felt the same at three in the morning.

"Who," he said.

"Someone you trust," Grey Sentinel said. "And someone who is running out of time."

Carrick didn't speak until they were in the car, headed back through the outskirts of Geneva with the windows up and the radio off.

"Believe him?" he said.

Avril looked at the road. "I believe they're not lying about what they know. Whether they're telling us all of it is a different question."

"The woman's files."

"If they're real, they change things."

"If." Carrick was quiet for a moment. "The younger one knows his material. The way he described the targeting architecture — that's not something you assemble from open source." Another pause. "Shoulder's been better, by the way. In case you were going to ask."

Avril looked at him. It was the first time Carrick had mentioned the Bellington wound since it happened. Avril had been watching him compensate for it for weeks — the weight shift, the way he favored the left side when coming through doorways, the particular economy of movement when he thought no one was watching. He had not said anything because Carrick had not said anything, and the rule between them, established without discussion, was that the wound existed operationally and not personally until Carrick decided otherwise.

"Good," Avril said.

"So that you know."

They drove the rest of the way without speaking. Avril kept his hands flat on his knees and thought about the name and the eight weeks and what it meant to be a liability to the people who had built the machine that was watching all of them.

Wrecker was in the safehouse kitchen when they got back, which was where Avril had half-expected to find him and also hadn't expected at all. He was making tea — actual tea, loose leaf, in a pot that had no business being in a safehouse kitchen — with the focused attention of someone who had learned that small rituals were the difference between functional and not.

He'd been gone for six weeks without explanation, which was the kind of thing that didn't get asked about directly in rooms like this one. What Avril knew: a wrong-house incident two years before the network existed, a man who had been in the wrong place with the wrong people for reasons that made sense at the time and stopped making sense later. What the incident had cost him. What staying had cost him since.

He looked up when Avril came in. Said nothing. Poured a second cup and set it on the counter without being asked.

Avril picked it up. It was better tea than the situation warranted.

"You're back," Avril said.

"Needed some time," Wrecker said. The cadence was the same as always — measured, final, nothing offered beyond what was asked for. "I'm back now."

That was all. Avril understood it was all. He drank the tea.

Mason had a briefing ready — two items, which meant he'd already filtered out everything that didn't require Avril's attention. The first was operational: a signal from a European routing cluster that someone in their benefactor network had flagged as significant. A series of encrypted queries, their origin masked behind three layers of commercial VPN, probed the edges of their infrastructure without crossing into it. Exploratory, not hostile. The kind of thing a government-adjacent actor did when trying to understand something without officially acknowledging curiosity.

"European?" Avril said.

"Almost certainly. The traffic pattern matches treaty-zone protocols. Old ones — infrastructure that predates the current surveillance architecture." Mason set the tablet down. "Someone with resources and a reason to stay off the record is trying to figure out if we're real."

"And whether we're stable."

"And whether we're stable," Mason agreed.

The second item was Jordan Myers. He had submitted a second application — not through the primary channel, but through a legacy address that had been inactive for eight months. Which meant he'd been watching long enough to know it existed. Which meant either he was extraordinarily patient and thorough, or he was extraordinarily patient and thorough for a reason.

"What did the application say?" Avril asked.

"Three sentences. 'I know you're evaluating me. I'd evaluate myself too. I'll wait.'" Mason paused. "I didn't know whether to find that reassuring or not."

"Neither do I," Avril said. "Leave it open."

He found Eliana in the room they'd been using as a library, which was four shelves of mismatched paperbacks someone had accumulated over years of other people passing through. She was reading something in Spanish — reading it, not pretending to, her attention fully inside the page. She looked up when Avril came in with the expression of someone who had been waiting for the conversation they were about to have.

"How did it go?" she said. Not a question.

He told her. The woman with the treaty compliance files. The younger man and the targeting architecture and the distinction between monitor and action. The eight weeks. The name he hadn't said aloud to anyone.

Eliana listened without interrupting, which was how she handled things that mattered. When he finished, she was quiet for a moment.

"They knew your name," she said. "Before the network launched." She looked at him. "I told you they knew someone else's, too."

"I know."

"Have you warned her?"

The question sat between them. He didn't answer, which was its own answer. Eliana didn't push. She had raised the question because she needed to raise it, and he had heard it, and that was what the silence meant.

"Grey Sentinel's two people," she said. "The files."

"If they're real."

"If." She closed her book. "Someone needs to verify them. Someone who isn't us — someone with standing. A journalist, maybe. Someone who can't be disappeared without consequence."

"Trina Cole used to be that person," Avril said.

Eliana looked at him carefully. "Used to be."

"I still have her number," he said. It was true in both the literal sense and the other sense, the one they both understood. The matchbook was in his jacket pocket, the corner still torn off. He'd been carrying it so long it had started to feel like part of the jacket.

"The question isn't whether you have it," Eliana said. "The question is what you're waiting for."

She picked her book back up. The conversation was over, which was also how she handled things that mattered.

That night, late, Avril sat at the table with the PERSISTENT/RED folder open and the name visible and the city quiet outside. He thought about action status and eight weeks and the difference between a threat inside the network and a threat to someone who had been in the network's orbit without ever choosing to be.

He thought about Lena.

He took the matchbook out of his pocket and set it on the table next to the laptop. Looked at them both for a long time. The corner was torn off cleanly, the way someone did when they wanted you to know they'd been there.

He thought about what Trina had looked like the last time he'd seen her — the way her eyes had gone flat, the particular quality of someone reading from a script they hated and had decided they couldn't afford to stop reading. The warning she'd given him anyway, in the thirty seconds between the script and the parking lot.

They're watching patterns now. Not just content — intent.

Intent.

He picked up the matchbook. He'd been treating it like a decision he hadn't made yet. He understood now that it was wrong. It had stopped being a decision somewhere in the middle of the weeks since she'd given it to him. It had become a fact he was choosing not to act on, which was different.

He put it in the inside pocket of his jacket, closer than the outside. He didn't use it tonight — but he moved it. He sat for another moment in the quiet of the late safehouse, and then something Grey Sentinel had said came back to him — not the name, not the eight weeks, but the other thing, the one he'd filed and not yet opened before you decided to build the network. Not before the network launched. Before he decided, he'd been so focused on the name — on the person the machine had moved to action status — that he'd glossed over the implication of those four words. If someone had known about the decision before he made it public, before the first post, before he'd told anyone what he was building — that wasn't surveillance. That was something embedded before the beginning. Something that had been inside the infrastructure since before there was an infrastructure to be inside. The SHADOW document was behind three authentication layers on his laptop. He opened it and added a fifth entry. He didn't sleep at all.

Outside, Geneva made its quiet sounds. He thought about Lina Alvarez, twenty-seven, and the twenty-three seconds of footage, and her name called out as the van doors closed. He thought about how the book he'd been building had started there, with that name, and how everything since had been an attempt to build something worthy of the reason she'd been taken.

He closed the folder.

Chapter Ten: Bellington

They were four minutes inside the drone window when Daniels found the flag.

"We have a problem," he said. Two seconds of silence first — the silence of someone running a calculation they don't want to finish.

"Define problem," Carrick said from the node terminal, not looking up.

"Active monitoring queue. Local organizer, name cross-referenced to three We Resist posts and a mutual aid network in Bellington proper." Daniels' fingers moved across the deck. "She's been flagged for forty-eight hours. Pickup order issued this morning, not yet executed."

Carrick looked up then. He looked at Daniels, then at the terminal, then at the countdown on his wrist. Three minutes forty seconds.

"She's not in the facility?" Avril asked.

"No. She's at home. We have her address from the queue metadata." Daniels paused. "We have everything. The flag, the criteria, the order. It's all on the drive."

The drive was already in Soto's coat. Thirty gigabytes of the regime's private architecture, the thing they'd come for, the thing that would take weeks to verify and months to matter.

"We can't reach her in three minutes," Carrick said.

"No," Daniels agreed.

"We can't abort and regroup. The window closes in—" he checked his wrist "—three thirty. We come back, we're building against a facility that knows it was hit."

"I know."

The ventilation cycled. Somewhere above them, a drone passed on its sweep arc and moved on.

"Her name," Avril said.

Daniels looked at him. "Nadia Voss. Thirty-one. She runs a food distribution network in the south quarter. Three kids. The flag is on her for—" he read it "—facilitating unsanctioned community assembly." He said the last four words the way you said something that tasted wrong.

The countdown read three minutes twelve.

Carrick said, "We go with what we came for."

Nobody argued. It was the right call, and they all knew it, and none of them liked it. Avril committed Nadia Voss's name to a part of his mind that kept things he hadn't decided what to do with yet.

"Moving," Soto said.

The exit was supposed to be clean. It was clean until the last forty meters, when a motion sensor Daniels had masked with a protocol loop cycled back faster than his model predicted, and a security drone dropped from its rail on Sublevel One.

Carrick took the round in his right shoulder — a glancing impact, not a clean hit, but enough to shunt him sideways into the wall. He kept moving. He didn't say anything. Avril only knew because of the way Carrick's left hand shifted to brace against the corridor wall at the next corner, with weight redistributed, the particular adjustment of someone who had learned to compensate for injury mid-operation and had done it before.

They reached the van. Daniels pulled the hatch. Soto got Carrick in first.

The city swallowed them the way it always did — without interest, without ceremony, just another vehicle. Three days later, Daniels found her name in the decrypted files.

They'd been working through the drive-in sections — verifying chains of custody, cross-referencing against public records, building the evidentiary architecture that would make the data useful rather than just true. It was slow, careful work. The kind Avril was good at.

He was the one who reached the monitoring queue section. He was the one who opened the active flags folder. He already knew what he was going to find.

VOSS, NADIA R. STATUS: DETAINED FACILITY: REGIONAL HOLDING 7 DATE: 72 HRS POST-FLAG

He read it twice. The timestamp put the detention fourteen hours after they'd cleared the Bellington perimeter. She'd been home when the pickup order was executed. Her food distribution network was listed in the detention notes as a secondary target for disruption. There was no mention of her children.

He opened a new file. He began building her case: the flag, the criteria, the detention record, the network's documented work, the community testimony he could gather remotely. He cross-referenced her name against the We Resist submissions that had been sitting in the inbox. Three of them mentioned her by first name — Nadia — as someone who showed up, who stayed, who could be counted on.

He added her to the archive. It was not enough. He did it anyway, because the alternative was leaving her name in a system that had decided she didn't matter, and he was not willing to do that.

Carrick's shoulder had been dressed by Soto — clean exit, no arterial involvement, the kind of wound that hurt for weeks and healed in months. He was sitting at the safehouse table with his arm in a sling he'd already taken off once and been told to put back on, reviewing the drive index with his good hand.

Avril sat across from him. He didn't say anything for a moment. Then:

"We had her name."

"Yes," Carrick said.

"We had the address. The forty-eight-hour window. We knew."

"We had three minutes and twelve seconds and a drone sweep that was already cycling back." Carrick turned a page in the index. "I made the call I had the information to make."

"I know," Avril said.

"The drive is real. The data is clean. What's on it is going to matter to a lot of people." Carrick looked at him then, directly. "That's nothing."

"No," Avril said. "It's nothing."

He thought about how Nadia Voss had run a food distribution network in the south quarter and been taken fourteen hours after they left. He thought about three kids whose names he didn't have. He thought about how the archive held her name now, correctly documented, provenance intact, admissible — and how none of that was the same as her being home.

Carrick went back to the index. Neither of them said anything else.

Avril went back to the file. He added one more entry: the names of her children, sourced from a community message board that hadn't been scrubbed yet. He didn't know why exactly. So the record would have it. So, the record would know.

Chapter Eleven: Deep Contact

The NSA Advisor had been awake since before the intercept, which was not unusual. Sleep had become a managed resource, taken in increments between signals.

The analyst who brought it to her desk said nothing when he set it down. He had learned to read her silences well enough to know that commentary would not be welcome. She read it once, then again, then set it flat on the blotter.

The routing was a dead channel — one her counterintelligence division had been monitoring without result for nineteen months. The handle was SABLE_VERITY. She knew the name. It had surfaced once before, as a metadata ghost embedded in the Unnamed File: someone who had touched the data before it reached We Resist. Someone who had, at some point, been inside.

She understood immediately what the transmission meant. Not a leak. A defection in progress.

She thought about what that would cost, and what it would cost not to stop it, and she thought about both of those things for a long time before she picked up the phone.

The message arrived at the safehouse terminal at 4:40 in the morning, routed through three relays and a dark-grid forum that had been dormant since February. Avril had been at the table anyway — he was always at the table now, in the hours before dawn, the PERSISTENT/RED folder open beside whatever else he was working on.

The decryption passphrase resolved it cleanly. Then the screen held the following:

FROM: [SABLE_VERITY]

PROTOCOL: ECHO-TWELVE

MESSAGE: YOU'VE DRAWN EYES. NOT ALL ARE HOSTILE. SOME REMEMBER THE OATH — NOT THE MAN. WE SEE YOUR FILE. WE FOLLOWED ITS TRAIL. WE WANT TO MEET.

He read it three times. Then he sat back and looked at the ceiling for a moment, which was something he did when he needed to think without looking at anything in particular.

SABLE_VERITY. He pulled up the Unnamed File index and found it in twelve seconds — a metadata ghost, a single handshake echo, consistent with systems used by a specific U.S. intelligence enclave. Someone who had handled the data before it reached him. Someone who had decided, at some point between then and now, that handling it wasn't enough.

He went and knocked on Carrick's door.

By seven in the morning, the core of the team was gathered, and the message had been read by everyone who needed to read it. Carrick stood near the window, the way he always did.

Reyes had his arms crossed. Mason was quiet in the corner, which meant he was paying closer attention than anyone else in the room.

It was Eliana who put the first question on the table.

"DIA protocol signature," she said. "Someone could have pulled that from a legacy archive. We've seen cleaner bait."

"But the metadata ghost in the Unnamed File is real," Avril said. "That's not something you construct after the fact. Whoever this is touched the data before it reached us."

"Which means they had access," Reyes said. "Which means they could also be running a trace."

"Or they're running out of time," Eliana said, "and this is the only channel they trust."

Carrick turned from the window. "Send a test. Something only a real insider would know. If they pass it, we talk. If they don't, we burn the channel and move."

The room absorbed that without objection.

Avril said, "I have something."

The test was a single question, sent back through the same routing:

TO: [SABLE_VERITY]

MESSAGE: Do you remember what happened at Tower Sentinel, July 7th?

The reply came eleven minutes later:

FROM: [SABLE_VERITY]

MESSAGE: I was there. The flare was not accidental. We all knew.

Avril read it twice. Carrick read it over his shoulder without being asked.

"She passes," Carrick said.

It was the first time anyone had used the pronoun. Avril noted it and said nothing.

Her name — her real name — was not something she used anymore. Within the remnants of the program she had built and then watched be repurposed, she was SABLE_VERITY, and that was sufficient. She had been the agency's architect of cognitive threat assessment: fluent in chaos modeling, trusted by the Joint Intelligence Committee, and cleared several levels above the people who signed off on black bag operations. The kind of career that only exists in the dark.

Tower Sentinel had been the line.

Not the mission itself — the mission, in the abstract, had precedents she could name and file numbers she could cite. What Tower Sentinel had been was a domestic operation: a coordinated program to discredit and neutralize a coalition of civil liberties lawyers, investigative journalists, and community organizers who were getting too close to the surveillance architecture. Not foreign adversaries. American citizens, on American soil, targeted under a classification so deep that the oversight mechanisms designed to catch exactly this kind of thing had themselves been compartmented away from it.

July 7th was the night it almost went further than surveillance and discreditation.

The target was a safe house: a group of journalists coordinating what would have been the largest domestic surveillance leak in a generation. The operation called for physical interdiction — not arrest, the kind that didn't produce paperwork. The flare was the abort signal, triggered by someone inside who had seen the order and decided in the time it took to reach for a flare gun. It bought the journalists one night. They moved. The window closed. Tower Sentinel was quietly reclassified, and the people who had been in that room with her were reassigned, retired, or disappeared into sealed programs with names she was never given.

She had stayed. She told herself it was to watch — to document, to understand the shape of the thing, to wait for a moment when the documentation could become something. A friend who pushed too hard on an ethics inquiry suffered what the agency called a breakdown and what she recognized as an engineered end to a career. Another was found in a river outside Reston and ruled a suicide. Full inbox. Secured future.

The silence around Tower Sentinel was not bureaucratic. It was enforced.

When the Unnamed File surfaced — when she recognized its architecture, understood that someone outside the machine had assembled something she had spent three years trying to assemble from inside it — she understood what she was looking at. The journalists from July 7th had never stopped. They'd changed form. Changed names. Built something decentralized enough that it couldn't be taken down the way a safe house could be taken down.

We Resist was the continuation of the thing that had been interrupted on July 7th. That made it, in a way she had stopped trying to articulate, an obligation.

She had been watching them for eight months before she sent the message.

The meet took three days to arrange and another two to vet. Avril insisted on the protocol: she would come alone, to a location she didn't choose, with a two-hour window and no recording devices that either side could confirm. She agreed to all of it without negotiation, which Carrick flagged and which Avril understood to mean either that she was exactly who she said she was or that she was very good.

The location was a reading room in the municipal library of a mid-sized city, which none of them had used before. Avril arrived forty minutes early. Carrick was already there.

She came in on time. She was in her mid-fifties, compact, with the stillness of someone who had spent decades being careful in rooms where being noticed was a professional failure. She sat down across from Avril and put nothing on the table.

"You already know I'm not going to tell you my name," she said.

"I know you were in the room on July 7th," Avril said. "I know you've had access to our architecture for at least eight months without doing anything damaging with it. And I know you sent the message on a channel that cost you something to use." He looked at her. "Those things tell me enough to be here."

She studied him the way people did when they were deciding how much truth to offer. "Tower Sentinel didn't end on July 7th," she said. "It was reclassified and restructured. What it became is the direct operational ancestor of the surveillance program currently active against your network. The procurement documentation that your Geneva contact has — the treaty compliance files — I can verify them. I can also fill in what they don't show."

Avril kept his face still. "What don't they show?"

"The domestic targeting list," she said. "The mechanism for moving people from monitor status to action status. And the name of the person inside your network who was moved to action eight weeks ago — not because they betrayed you, but because of what they know about Tower Sentinel's current iteration." She paused. "They witnessed something. The agency knows they witnessed it. They've been deciding what to do about it longer than you know."

The room was quiet. Somewhere in the stacks, a door closed softly.

Avril thought about the PERSISTENT/RED folder and the name at the top of it and all the months of watching someone he trusted through the lens of suspicion. He thought about how different those two things were — betrayal and exposure — and how much the distinction mattered now.

"Who," he said.

She looked at him steadily. "Someone you haven't warned yet," she said. "Someone who is running out of time for you to do it."

He told Carrick in the car. Carrick listened without interrupting, which was how he handled things that changed the shape of what they were doing. When Avril finished, Carrick was quiet for a long time.

"Eliana will want to verify the files before anything else," he said finally.

"I know."

"Reyes will want to know how she got access to our architecture without triggering anything."

"I know."

Another silence. Outside, the city moved past in the early afternoon light — ordinary, indifferent, busy with things that had nothing to do with any of this.

"The name," Carrick said. "She gave it to you."

"She gave it to me."

"And?"

Avril looked at the road. He thought about Lena's name on the watchlist and the matchbook in his inside pocket and the quality of the sleeplessness that had been his companion for months. He thought about what it meant that he had been watching the wrong thing.

"I have to warn her," he said. "Tonight."

Carrick said nothing. That was its own kind of answer.

Back at the safehouse, Avril sat at the table for a long time before he opened anything. The PERSISTENT/RED folder. The Unnamed File. The matchbook was taken out of his pocket and set on the table in front of him.

Lena.

He thought about what Eliana had asked him, twice now: Have you warned her? He thought about the silence that had been his answer both times. He thought about action status and eight weeks and what that interval meant in terms of how much time was left before the answer stopped mattering.

He thought about Lina Alvarez. Twenty-seven. A civics teacher. Her name was called out as the van doors closed. The twenty-three seconds of footage that had made him build the thing that had brought all of this to this table, to this night, to this decision he had been refusing to make.

He picked up the matchbook.

He opened it.

He looked at the number written inside — Trina Cole's number, in her own handwriting, the corner torn off so he would know she'd been there. He thought about what she'd looked like the last time he'd seen her. Eyes flat. Reading from a script. And the thirty seconds in the parking lot when she'd stopped.

Two things. Both tonight.

He reached for his phone.

Chapter Twelve: The Great Divide

The call she had placed the night before had taken eleven minutes to connect and thirty seconds to resolve. The man on the other end of it had not wasted words, which was why she used him. He had confirmed one thing she already knew and told her one thing she didn't, and the one thing she didn't know had kept her at her desk through the night and into a gray morning that arrived without apology.

She stood at the window with coffee she wasn't drinking and looked at the city below and thought about what it meant to watch something accelerate.

SABLE_VERITY's defection was in progress. That part she had read correctly from the transmission. What she had misread — what the thirty seconds on the phone had corrected — was the timeline. She had assumed weeks. The correction was days. Possibly less.

She set the coffee down. She thought about a civilian archivist in a safehouse somewhere in Europe, reaching for his phone in the dark. She thought about what he would say when he made the call he'd not been making for months, and who would answer, and what that conversation would set in motion.

She had three directives active. She had resources. She had the patience that came from understanding that rushing the wrong move cost more than waiting for the right one.

What she did not have was time.

She picked up the phone again.—

Avril had dialed the number three times before he let it connect.

The first time, he'd gotten as far as the second digit and stopped. The second time, he'd let it ring once and cut it. The third time, he sat very still and waited, and she picked up on the fourth ring with the particular flatness of someone who has been awake long enough that the hour has stopped meaning anything.

"It's me," he said.

A pause. Long enough to mean something. "I know," she said.

He had planned what he was going to say. He had planned it in the car from Geneva, at the table with the matchbook, and in the hour between deciding and dialing. None of it was available to him now. What came out was the only true version.

"You're on a list," he said. "A specific one. The kind that doesn't stay still."

Another pause. He heard her breathing change — not panic, something quieter than panic, the sound of someone adjusting to a weight they had always known might arrive. "How long?" she said.

"Six weeks that I know of. Probably longer." He closed his eyes. "I should have called sooner."

"Yes," she said. Just that. Not a condemnation, just a fact, offered and absorbed and set aside. That had always been her register when things were serious — the economy of someone who understood that anger was a resource and this wasn't the moment to spend it.

He told her what she needed to know. Not everything — not SABLE_VERITY, not the name of the person who had confirmed it, not the mechanics of the targeting architecture. What she needed: that the monitoring was active, that it was not about what she had done but about what she knew, and that she needed to move. Somewhere she hadn't been before. Someone she hadn't contacted in more than a year.

"The scarf," she said, when he'd finished.

He didn't understand for a moment. Then he did. It was in the inside pocket of his jacket, where it had been for months — cedar and ink, the smell of it faint now but still there. She'd left it for him to have something to hold when the fear arrived. It had never occurred to him that she'd been calculating the same thing about herself.

"I have it," he said.

"Good," she said. And then: "Don't call this number again."

The line went quiet. He sat with the phone in his hand for a long time after.

The second call was different. He had expected it to be harder, and it wasn't, which itself was a kind of hard.

Trina picked up on the second ring. He hadn't announced himself — the number would have told her everything. There was a silence, and then she said: "You finally opened it."

"I opened it," he said.

Another silence, and in it he could hear the calculation she was running — how much time she had, who might be on the line with her, what the cost of this conversation would be against what it might buy. He recognized it because he ran the same calculation himself now, automatically, the way you learned to check exits when you walked into a room.

"I can't do this on an open channel," she said.

"I know. I'm not asking you to." He had thought about how to say the next part. He'd settled on direct. "There are documents. Treaty compliance files, procurement records, and provenance chains that would hold up to forensic review. The people who have them need someone with standing to verify them. Someone who can't be —" He stopped.

"Disappeared without consequence," she said. Flat. Clinical. The way you named a thing you'd spent a long time learning to look at directly.

"Yes."

She was quiet for long enough that he began to calculate whether the line had gone dead. Then: "Where."

"I'll send you a routing. A dead-drop address, one use. You'll need —"

"I know what I'll need." A pause that carried the weight of the last time they'd been in the same room — the flat eyes, the script, the thirty seconds in the parking lot that had cost her something she'd chosen not to name. "Avril. The people who have these files. Are you certain of them?"

He thought about SABLE_VERITY in the library reading room, compact and still, putting nothing on the table. He thought about what it had cost her to send the message on a channel that cost her something to use.

"As certain as I am of anything," he said.

She said: "That's not very certain."

"No," he agreed. "It isn't."

A last silence. Then: "Send the routing. I'll look at what they have." She paused. "And Avril. They're watching patterns now. Intent, not content. You know what that means for a call like this one."

"I know," he said.

The line went quiet. He thought about what she'd looked like the last time he'd seen her — the flatness that had been a kind of survival, the thirty seconds that had been a kind of resistance, and the matchbook that had been both. He thought about how long she'd been carrying the cost of what she knew without anyone to carry it with.

He put the phone down and sat in the dark for a while, listening to the building settle.

He told Eliana first. She was already in the library — or she had been there long enough that it amounted to the same thing — sitting with a book open on her knees that she wasn't reading. She looked up when he came in with the expression of someone who had been waiting for the conversation they were about to have.

"Lena," she said. Not a question.

"Last night." He sat down across from her. "She's moving."

Eliana was quiet for a moment. She closed the book. "And Trina?"

"She'll look at the files."

Something shifted in Eliana's face — not relief, something more cautious. An adjustment. "She understood what we're asking."

"She understood before I finished the sentence."

Eliana looked at him steadily. "How did it go. The call to Lena."

He thought about the way Lena's breathing had changed. The economy of her. Don't call this number again. "She's handled worse," he said.

"That's not what I asked."

He looked at the shelves. The mismatched paperbacks, accumulated across years of other people passing through — other rooms, other urgencies, the same slow accumulation of things that needed to be survived. "It went the way it had to," he said.

Eliana let the silence sit for a moment, which was how she held things that didn't need more words. Then: "Mason has something. When you're ready."

"I'm ready."

She stood, and for a moment she just looked at him — the particular attention of someone who was measuring something she wasn't going to say. Whatever she found, she seemed to find it sufficient. She moved toward the door.

"Eliana," he said.

She stopped.

"The other question," he said. "The one you've not been asking."

She turned. Her expression was careful. "I've been asking it."

"The one before that."

A beat. She understood. She gave him the slight nod of someone who had been carrying a question for long enough that having it acknowledged was enough. She didn't say: I told you so, or: I was right, or: it's good you finally moved. She just nodded. And that was all it needed to be.

Mason had two items, which meant he'd filtered. He led with the one that could wait and closed with the one that couldn't, which was how Avril knew it was serious before he got to it.

The first was the European traffic. The quiet probing of their infrastructure from government-adjacent sources had continued — same treaty-zone protocols, same careful edges, same quality of something deciding whether to trust. Someone was closer to deciding. Mason had flagged two specific queries that suggested they were trying to understand not just whether We Resist was real, but whether it was intact.

"They've seen something that spooked them," Mason said. "Or heard something. They want to know if we're still standing."

"We're still standing," Avril said.

"I know." Mason set the tablet down. "They don't."

The second item was Jordan Myers. He had sent nothing new — no message, no query, no attempt to make contact through any channel. The legacy address he'd used for the second application had gone quiet. Which was either patience or tradecraft, and the distance between those two things was the problem.

"He said he'd wait," Avril said.

"He's waiting." Mason folded his hands in the way he did when he was offering an observation without offering a verdict. "Waiting is a skill. Some people are born with it. Some people are trained to it."

"Leave it open," Avril said.

Mason nodded once. That was all.

There was a third item. Mason had held it because he wasn't sure what to do with it, which was unusual enough that Avril noticed the pause before he raised it.

"It came through SABLE_VERITY's channel," he said. "A contact request. Handle I don't recognize — six characters, J.E_127. No preamble, no context. Just a question: had we seen the footage of the woman in Cincinnati?"

Avril looked at him. "And had we?"

"Not yet," Mason said. "I've queued it. Whatever it is, it came through a channel that cost something to use, which means someone thinks it matters."

"Pull the footage," Avril said. "Tonight."

Mason nodded and left without further comment, which was how he handled things that were about to become something.

He found Carrick in the kitchen, standing at the counter with a cup of coffee and the particular stillness of someone who had been there long enough to have processed what they needed to process. The shoulder was better — Avril could see it in the way he was standing, the slight return of a posture that had been compensating for months.

"You made the calls," Carrick said. Not a question.

"Last night."

"Lena's moving?"

"She's moving."

Carrick turned the cup in his hands. "Trina Cole."

"She'll look at the files. I'm sending the routing today."

A silence. Outside, the morning was doing what mornings did — arriving without asking whether the people inside it were ready. Carrick drank his coffee. He looked out the window for a moment at nothing in particular, the way people did when they were cataloguing something they weren't going to say aloud.

"The NSA Advisor intercepted SABLE_VERITY's transmission," Avril said. "She knows the contact happened."

"I know," Carrick said.

"She made a call last night. We don't know to whom."

"I know that too."

Another silence. Carrick set the cup down. He looked at Avril with the flat directness that meant he was about to say the thing he'd been deciding whether to say.

"The warning to Lena," he said. "It was the right call. It was also six weeks late."

"I know."

"I'm not—" He stopped. Reconsidered. "That's not a criticism. That's a statement of the gap between knowing what needs doing and being able to do it." He picked up the cup again. "We're going to keep running into that gap. The closer this gets, the more often."

Avril thought about the PERSISTENT/RED folder and the months of watching someone he'd been wrong about. He thought about all the things he'd been not-doing for the exact reason Carrick was describing, and what each deferred action had cost in time and exposure and the particular anguish of someone who suspects and cannot yet prove.

"I know," he said, for the third time.

Carrick nodded once. That was sufficient. He picked up his coffee and turned back toward the window, and the conversation was over, which was how Carrick ended things when they were done.

Late afternoon. The safehouse quieted in the way it did when the team had dispersed into their separate work — Mason at his terminal, Eliana reading something in the library that she was actually reading this time, Wrecker somewhere with his small rituals. The building breathed.

Avril sat at the table with the PERSISTENT/RED folder open and Trina Cole's matchbook beside it. Both things he'd been carrying for months. Both things that had stopped being deferred and started being facts. He thought about how different those two states were — a decision unmade versus a decision in motion — and how much lighter one was than the other.

He pulled the scarf from his jacket pocket. Cedar and ink. The smell was fainter than it had been — months of being carried had worn it down to something you had to want to find. But it was there.

He thought about Lena, somewhere she hadn't been before, establishing the invisibility she should have been establishing six weeks ago. He thought about how quickly and quietly she had taken what he'd told her and begun to move. The economy of her. The absence of accusation. He thought about what it cost to be that composed when composure was the only option left.

He thought about Lina Alvarez. Twenty-seven. The twenty-three seconds. Her name was called out as the van doors closed. The footage that had made him build the thing that had brought all of this — the Porto cottage and the Geneva archive and the library in the mid-sized city and SABLE_VERITY and Trina

Cole and the matchbook and the scarf — to this table, to this afternoon, to this particular quality of exhaustion that wasn't defeat.

The book he was building had started with her name. Everything since had been an attempt to be worthy of the reason she'd been taken. He didn't know if he was succeeding. He suspected that was the wrong question. The right question was whether he was still trying, and the answer to that was the same as it had been the night he'd first opened the folder.

He put the scarf back. He opened the routing protocol for Trina Cole's dead drop. He began to build it, carefully, one layer at a time, the way you built anything that had to hold weight.

Outside, the city made its ordinary sounds. Somewhere in it, the machine was watching patterns. Somewhere in it, a woman was moving from one invisible life toward another, carrying nothing she didn't have to. The routing took forty minutes. He checked it twice. Then he sent it.

Then he sat back and let the afternoon go quiet around him, and thought about what it meant that two things he had been not-doing for months were now done, and what would be required of him next, and whether he was ready. He wasn't. He knew that. He also knew it didn't matter. He left the folder open. He waited for whatever the morning would bring.

Chapter Thirteen: Extraction Orders

The person she had called was not someone she called lightly. That was what the eleven minutes of routing had meant — not technical caution, though there was that, but the particular weight of reaching for a resource you conserve precisely because using it costs something that doesn't come back.

He had told her two things. The first, she had already known, confirmed now with a precision that moved it from intelligence to fact. The second was a location. A site outside Louisville, federal land on paper, operating under a name she recognized as one of seven active designations in a program she had spent three years ensuring remained invisible to congressional oversight.

She stood at the window with the city below her and understood that the situation had changed shape overnight. Not because of anything We Resist had done — not yet. Because of what SABLE_VERITY had given them, and what they would do with it if she didn't move first.

She had three directives active. She had resources. What she did not have was the luxury of waiting for the right moment.

She picked up the phone.

Not them, she said, when he answered. The site. If they're moving toward it, the site has to change first.

A pause. Then: Understood.

She hung up. She thought about a civilian archivist somewhere in Europe, pulling footage of a woman in Cincinnati. She thought about what he would find and how long it would take him to decide what to do with it. She was good at calculating those intervals. She had been doing it for months.

She did not think it would be long.

Mason had pulled the footage by the time Avril came back to the table. He'd said nothing — just turned the screen so it was visible and stepped back.

A sidewalk outside a federal courthouse. Afternoon light. A woman with a handmade sign, crayon lettering across the bottom in a child's hand. Beside her, two children, and the sign she was holding read something Avril couldn't make out fully before the angle shifted. Two unmarked vehicles arrived after the ambient light changed. The woman and the children were escorted away without visible force — calmly, efficiently, in the manner of something that had been rehearsed.

Forty-seven seconds of footage. Then nothing.

Her name, Avril said.

Naomi Ellis, Mason said. Husband is Carlos Ellis. Department of Energy data analyst. He flagged an infrastructure audit report as incomplete — sent a follow-up to oversight. The system logged the upload as failed. Two weeks later, the family was gone. No charges. No public record. Her sister has been trying to find them for six weeks.

The sister is J.E_127.

Yes. Mason set a tablet on the table. She reached out through SABLE_VERITY's channel last night, after you'd gone. I didn't want to add it to the pile, but — he paused, — I looked at the footage, and I thought you should see it yourself.

Avril looked at the frozen frame. The sign. The children. Where are they, he said. Not a question.

SABLE_VERITY has a location. Mason glanced at the door, then back. She's been watching a site outside Louisville for three weeks. Something changed in the last forty-eight hours — vehicle activity, power draw. She thinks they're going to be moved.

Avril sat back. He thought about the Bellington op, the CECOT extraction, the accumulated weight of each decision, and what it had cost the people who'd trusted them to make it correctly.

Bring Carrick, he said. And Reyes. Tonight.

The message came through on the secure terminal at eleven, routed through two dead relays. Avril read it twice standing up, then pulled a chair and read it again.

The paragraph below is the SABLE_VERITY message block — built separately.

Mason had printed the site schematic from the attachments: a cluster of buildings on federal land, square and utilitarian. No signage in the imagery. A chain-link perimeter, automated gates. And running from a utility station at the property's edge, a decommissioned maintenance tunnel, original construction early 1990s, noted in the site's own suppressed infrastructure records as sealed but intact.

She's been inside their files, Reyes said, from across the table. He was looking at the schematic with the particular attention he gave to things that had to hold weight. That's not open-source. That's not leaked. Someone handed her internal records, or she was in the system long enough to pull them herself.

She was the architect, Avril said. She built some of this. She knows where the doors are because she drew the blueprints.

Reyes turned the schematic. Tunnel's the only entry point that doesn't put us on a camera before we're ready. Guard rotation — if the timing in here is current — gives us a window at the shift change. Thirty seconds, maybe forty.

If the timing is current, Eliana said.

If Reyes agreed, he didn't say more. He didn't need to.

Jessica Ellis came through on a voice-only line, her connection routed through the same channel her sister had used on the burner — a number that hadn't existed until six weeks ago and would stop existing the moment this call ended. Her voice had the particular flatness of someone who had been frightened for long enough that the fear had become the baseline.

I've been followed, she said. Calls dropped mid-sentence. I opened a file — I didn't even say anything out loud, I just opened it — and the next morning, my employer locked me out of our internal system.

What file, Avril said.

Carlos's clearance revocation notice. I wanted to understand what he'd done that triggered it. That's all.

She had a voicemail. Naomi, a week before she disappeared, was on the burner. She played it through the line without being asked, and it came through as Avril had learned things like this always came through — in a voice that had been afraid and was trying not to sound it, for the sake of whoever was listening.

Jess. If you're hearing this, we've gone underground. Carlos flagged a report — said some numbers didn't add up on the infrastructure audits. He sent it to oversight, but the system crashed while uploading. Then someone from Homeland showed up. Said it was a miscommunication. But they knew the kids' school schedules, Jess. They knew. If something happens — don't let them say we disappeared. We didn't disappear. We were taken.

The line was quiet for a moment after it ended.

She has asthma, Jessica said. So do the kids. Severe. If they were relocated anywhere legitimately, she'd have insisted on prescription access. I checked every state medical portal. Not a single fill since she vanished. Not an ER visit. Nothing. A pause. They're not in the system anymore.

What did Carlos mean by 'the infrastructure audits,' Eliana said. Did he specify which system?

He called it Layer Nine, Jessica said. I thought it was technical jargon. Naomi used it too, like it was code for something they both understood. I don't know what it means.

Avril looked at Mason across the table. Mason was already writing it down.

Jessica sent a file before the call ended — a floor plan, partial, sourced from someone in her church who had worked for the contractor that wired the sublevel. Badge checkpoint positions. HVAC access. The tunnel entry was marked in handwriting that wasn't an engineer's.

Move soon, she said. I think they're going to transfer them.

Why.

Because there's been a black SUV outside my building for the last five hours.

Eliana reached across and ended the call before anyone asked whether she was safe. The answer was already in the room.

Daniels had the term in twenty minutes. He'd heard it once, in the context of a compartmentalized DoD framework, in a document that had been pulled from a review server before the review completed. He laid it out without editorializing, which was how he handled things that were worse than he wanted them to be.

Layer Nine was an informal designation, he said. For operations structured specifically to avoid generating FOIA-accessible records. Not just classified — architecturally invisible. The procurement runs through contractors. The contractors run through subsidiaries. By the time you get to the money, you're four entities away from anything that looks like government action.

Is there a paper trail, Avril asked.

There's the absence of one, Daniels said. Which, if you know what you're looking at, is its own kind of document. He glanced at Eliana. The procurement records Grey Sentinel's contact is holding — the treaty compliance files — I think they're describing the same architecture from the outside. Trina Cole is going to find the match.

The room absorbed that for a moment.

Then the Ellis family isn't a separate thread, Eliana said. She said it quietly, the way she said things that had weight. They're inside the same structure. Carlos found a seam in Layer Nine and pulled on it, and that's why they're gone.

Nobody disagreed.

Carrick had been listening from the doorway for some of this, which Avril had learned was how Carrick processed things he hadn't decided on yet. When he came fully into the room, he did it the way he did everything — without announcement, with the settled weight of someone who had already run the calculation and arrived at a position.

U.S. soil is different, he said.

It wasn't a question or an objection. It was a statement of operating conditions, offered to the room as a fact to be worked with.

CECOT was an allied jurisdiction, he continued. Legally complicated, operationally complex, but there was a framework for what we were doing, even if the framework was bent. This — he gestured at the schematic — is a federal installation on American ground. If we go in and it goes wrong, we don't get to be the extraction team. We become the incident.

And if we don't go in, Eliana said.

Then a woman and her children stay in a facility that doesn't officially exist, for a reason that never gets filed, until someone decides what to do with them. Carrick looked at the floor plan for a moment. I'm not arguing against. I'm telling you what we're walking into so nobody's surprised when we get there.

Reyes had been marking the schematic while they talked. Tunnel approach keeps us off the camera grid until we're inside the perimeter. From the sublevel entry to the detention wing, it's forty meters of corridor. Guard shift change gives us a window — if the timing SABLE_VERITY pulled is still current.

How old is the data, Carrick asked.

Seventy-two hours.

Carrick nodded once. Then we plan for it to be different and adapt if it isn't. Small team. I lead entry. Reyes handles logistics. Eliana stays on the exterior line — if something changes on the perimeter, I need someone who can read it and make a call, not just report it.

Eliana looked at him. A civil rights attorney on the exterior line of a domestic extraction op. She didn't say anything about the distance between that and what she had been two years ago. She didn't need to.

What about Soto? Avril asked.

Soto drives, Carrick said. And she knows how to disappear a vehicle. He picked up the schematic. Give me two hours with this. Then we talk about what we're actually going to do.

Avril found Eliana in the library again, standing this time, looking at the mismatched spines on the shelves without appearing to read any of them. The files Trina's reviewing, he said. Daniels thinks they're going to confirm what the Ellis case already shows. Layer Nine, Tower Sentinel, the surveillance architecture — it's the same system at different stages.

I know, Eliana said. She turned. I've been thinking about what that means for the documentation strategy. If the files connect — if Trina can establish provenance from Grey Sentinel's records through to an active detention site — that's not a leak. That's a case.

We have to get them out first.

Yes. She looked at him steadily. And then we have to be ready for what comes after. Because getting them out isn't the end of it, it's the beginning of a different kind of exposure. She paused. Carrick's right about U.S. soil. I want you to know I understand what we're doing.

Do you want not to do it, Avril asked.

She looked at him for a moment — the particular look of someone being precise. No, she said. I want to do it knowing exactly what it is.

He nodded. That was all it needed.

He thought about Naomi Ellis's voice on the recording — the effort to sound steady, the school schedules, don't let them say we disappeared. He thought about Lina Alvarez, twenty-seven. Her name. The van doors. The twenty-three seconds that had made him build the thing that had brought all of them to this particular hallway, to this particular night, to a schematic on the table and a tunnel that might or might not still be clear.

He went to find Carrick.

Soto brought the vehicle around at midnight — a regional waterworks decal on the side, riding low, blacked out. She'd sourced it the same way she sourced everything: through a chain that ended far enough from any of them that tracing it back would take longer than the op.

Carrick ran a final check on the schematic. Reyes had the med kit and the comms. Eliana pulled the exterior position without being asked twice. Avril watched all of it from the doorway and thought about what Mason had said about the third item in the briefing — the one he hadn't been sure what to do with. Whatever it is, it came through a channel that cost something to use. Which means someone thinks it matters. Jessica Ellis had sent one more message through the secure relay, timestampless, before they'd left the safehouse: If I'm gone by the time you get back — tell them I tried.

No follow-up. Avril had read it and not responded, because there was nothing to say that the op itself wasn't already saying.

Carrick was already outside.

They stopped a mile from the facility. The access road was overgrown. Forest stillness — the particular silence that means everything in range is listening. Carrick crouched at the tunnel entrance and ran a light along the concrete slope without speaking. Reyes checked the comms unit's fit with the focus of someone who understood that the difference between a good seal and a bad one was the difference between this working and it not.

Thirty-second window, Carrick said. We're through before it closes.

He went first. The tunnel swallowed him. Reyes followed.

Avril stood at the edge of the slope for a moment, one foot on solid ground. He thought about the gap Carrick had named — between knowing what needs doing and being able to do it. He thought about how many times he had stood at the edge of something and calculated the cost of going against the cost of not going, and how the calculation had never gotten easier, and how that was probably right.

He went in.

Above them, Eliana held the exterior line, watching the perimeter cameras cycle through their rotation, counting the seconds between each sweep. She had a civil rights attorney's understanding of what they were doing and a civil rights attorney's knowledge of what happened when it went wrong.

She counted. She watched. She waited for the window.

Chapter Fourteen: The Plea

The report came in at 4:40 in the morning, which was the time reports like this one always came in. She read it standing at her desk. She did not sit down.

The site change had been ordered with twelve hours to spare. The transfer had been initiated on schedule. Somewhere in the execution — a guard rotation, a communications gap, a thirty-second window she didn't have the details on yet — the operation had been interrupted. The family had been partially extracted. The mother and children were gone. The father had been separated during loading and was now in transit to a secondary facility whose location had not yet been confirmed.

She set the report flat on the blotter.

They had been inside the transfer. Not surveilling it — inside it. On American soil, at a federal transfer operation, with enough operational intelligence to intercept a moving convoy in the dark. The civilian archivist she had been tracking for the better part of a year had just run an extraction op on a domestic detention transfer.

She thought about what that meant for the three directives she had been working on. She thought about the gap between what she had known and what she had underestimated.

She picked up the phone. This time, she did not route it. She dialed directly.

Find the father, she said, when it connected. And find out who gave them the rotation schedule.

The transfer vehicle had been a white panel van, government plates, running without lights on a service road that had no reason to exist on a civilian map. Carrick had identified it by the heat signature — two adult bodies in the rear compartment, two smaller ones, all of them still.

Still, not dead. That had been the first thing Avril had needed to know.

Reyes had taken the vehicle's front axle with a precision that left no room for anything except stopping — not a crash, not a rollover, just the particular violence of something being made to halt. The driver had not been expecting resistance. That was the only reason it had worked.

There were three personnel in the vehicle. Two in the cab, one in the rear with the family. Carrick had handled the cab. Avril had taken the rear door. What he found inside was four people zip-tied at the wrists, seated on a metal bench in a space designed for cargo, in the dark.

Naomi Ellis looked at him the way people looked when they had stopped believing anyone was coming. It took her a moment to understand what she was seeing.

Where's Carlos, she said—the first words out of her.

He hadn't been in the van. Avril had understood that before he finished scanning the compartment, and he'd understood what it meant — a second vehicle, a different route, a deliberate separation that someone had decided was prudent operational procedure for a family being moved in the middle of the night.

We're going to get you out first, Avril said.

She had looked at him for a moment with the expression of someone calculating whether the truth was in what he'd said or in what he hadn't. Then she had reached back for her children, and they had moved.

The window from intercept to clear was four minutes. Carrick had said three. They made it in four because one of the children couldn't walk without help and wouldn't let go of her mother's hand to take Avril's, and he hadn't tried to make her.

Soto had the vehicle running. They were gone before anyone with a radio had assembled a picture of what had happened.

In the back of the vehicle, on the way out, Avril had sat across from Naomi Ellis and her two children in the dark. The older one — a girl, maybe nine — had her face pressed against her mother's shoulder and was breathing in the careful, deliberate way of someone who had learned that panic cost her something she couldn't spare. He recognized it. He didn't say anything about it.

Nobody spoke for the first twenty minutes. That was right.

The drive back was five hours. Carrick sat in the front and didn't speak, which was how he processed things he was still deciding about. Reyes drove with the particular focus of someone working through contingencies in silence. Eliana was at the safehouse — she had held the exterior line, then stood down when they were clear, then been given the task of making a room safe for two children and their mother before any of them arrived.

It was the kind of task that looked like logistics and wasn't.

When they came through the door, the room was warm. There was food on the table that hadn't been there before. Eliana was standing near the window, and she looked at Naomi Ellis with the particular attention of someone who had spent years in courtrooms reading what people needed before they asked for it.

The children went to the food. Children, Avril had noticed, had a way of finding the ordinary thing in an extraordinary situation and moving toward it. He was always grateful for that.

Naomi sat down in the nearest chair. She hadn't stopped being composed — she was too experienced at fear to lose composure now — but something in her had reached a limit and was resting against it. She looked at Avril.

You didn't get him, she said.

Not yet, he said.

She absorbed that. The not-yet was the part that mattered — the acknowledgment that it was still a fact in motion rather than a closed one. She nodded once, the way people nodded when they were accepting the terms of something they hadn't chosen.

He'll know we're out, she said. That'll be enough for now. He'll know.

Avril didn't know whether that was true or whether it was what she needed it to be. He let it stand.

Eliana was already across the room with the older girl, talking quietly about something that had nothing to do with any of this — a book on the shelf, the color of the cover — and the girl was answering in a small voice that was becoming slightly less small. The younger one had fallen asleep against his sister with a piece of bread still in his hand.

Carrick stood in the doorway for a moment, looking at all of this. Then he went outside. Avril followed him.

The rotation schedule, Carrick said, when they were clear of the door. They're going to know someone had it.

I know.

Which means they're going to look at SABLE_VERITY.

I know.

Carrick looked at the dark for a moment. We need to move her, he said, before they close the gap.

It was the right call, and they both knew it. Avril thought about the stillness of SABLE_VERITY in the library reading room —

compact, careful, putting nothing on the table. He thought about what it cost to stay inside something for years, waiting for the right moment to hand it to someone who could use it. He thought about the river outside Reston.

Tonight, Avril said.

Carrick nodded. They went back inside.

Mason had found it at the drop point while they were in Louisville. He'd recognized the verification stamp and brought it back sealed, which was the correct procedure and also the mark of someone who understood when to hold a thing until the right moment.

The right moment, as he read the room, was not while Naomi Ellis was sitting ten feet away. He waited until she and the children had been moved to the back room, until the door was closed, until the safehouse had taken on the particular quiet of a place where people are sleeping for the first time in a long time.

Then he set it on the table in front of Avril.

It was a piece of paper, folded into quarters. The book it had come from was Don Quixote — a copy that had sat in the dead drop since the early days of the network. Avril recognized it the way you recognized something you'd placed somewhere deliberately and half-forgotten. He unfolded the paper.

The handwriting was clean, careful. Anonymous. The phrasing of someone who had thought about each word before committing it.

You don't know me. My name doesn't matter. What matters is that my cousin and her family are gone and deported without charges, without a hearing. Immigration lawyer. His wife is a teacher. Two daughters. The younger one — she uses a nebulizer every day. Has since she was three. I've tried every official channel. There are no channels left. I found you the only way I could. If you can help them, please. They are not criminals. They are just people.

There was a verification stamp on the inner fold — an encrypted one-time code from the early network, one Avril had issued personally to a small group of sympathizers in the first year. The kind of thing that was hard to forge and harder to explain unless you'd been there.

He read it twice. He set it down.

The word nebulizer sat in the room with everything else that was in the room.

He didn't say anything about it. He didn't need to. Eliana, who had come in from the back, had seen his face when he read it.

Another one, she said. Not a question.

Another one, he said.

They gathered late, in the way they gathered when something needed to be decided, but no one was sure yet what the deciding looked like. Carrick stood near the window. Reyes had the plea in his hand — he'd read it twice without expression, which was how he read things he was taking seriously. Daniels was at the terminal in the corner, already running the name without being asked. Mason had made tea again, which Avril had come to understand was how Mason marked the hours that mattered.

Deportation without a hearing, Carrick said. Emergency Enforcement Protocol. That's a designation that's been used seventeen times in the last eight months. Every single family flagged under it has an adult with a professional license or an institutional affiliation that someone found inconvenient. He said it without editorializing, the way he said everything. It's not random.

The verification code is clean, Daniels said from the corner, without looking up. Issued in the first year to a sympathizer in the Midwest. I can't confirm who's using it now without more time, but the code itself hasn't been burned.

'Can't confirm' is different from 'confirmed,' Reyes said.

Yes, Daniels said. It is.

Eliana had the plea in her hands now. She read it the way she read things she was going to have to say something difficult about. We just got back from Louisville, she said. Carlos Ellis is still in a secondary facility we haven't located. SABLE_VERITY needs to be moved tonight. Trina Cole is mid-verification on documents that could break this open at a structural level. She looked at the paper. We are not resourced for another extraction op. Not right now.

The room absorbed that. It was true.

I'm not proposing an extraction op, Avril said. Not yet. I'm proposing we find out whether these people are real and where they are. Those are different things.

Recon has a way of becoming commitment, Reyes said.

So does reading a piece of paper, Avril said.

A silence. Reyes looked at the floor. That was its own kind of answer.

The father is an immigration lawyer, Carrick said. If he was flagged under Emergency Enforcement Protocol, there's a reason. Not a legal one — a political one. Something he was working on, a case, a client, something that generated enough friction to get him moved. He paused. If we can find what that was, it connects to everything else we have. The procurement chain, the targeting list. This isn't a random family. This is the system doing what the system does.

It was the most Carrick had said in one sequence in weeks. The room understood what that meant.

Eliana set the plea on the table. Verify first, she said—all the way. If the code traces back and the family is real and the father's case connects to anything we already have, then we talk about next steps. She looked at Avril. But SABLE_VERITY moves tonight. That's not negotiable.

Agreed, Avril said.

Agreed, Carrick said.

Daniels was already typing.

Late. The safehouse had settled into the particular quiet of a building with more people in it than it was used to. Naomi Ellis and her children were in the back room. The older girl's breathing had evened out — Eliana had checked twice, without making a thing of it, and reported it to Avril with a single nod.

Avril sat at the table with the plea open in front of him. The verification had come back clean an hour ago. The father's name was Tomás Herrera — immigration attorney with three years of case filings for undocumented workers at a poultry processing plant in Arkansas. Two of his clients had testified before a state oversight committee; one of those clients had been a whistleblower on facility safety violations. The deportation order had been signed forty-eight hours after the testimony.

It connected. Not loosely — directly. The same procurement chain Daniels had traced from Layer Nine ran through the subsidiary that operated the poultry plant's private security contract. The same architecture. A different face. Grey Sentinel had sent something three days earlier — a fragment, routed through the secondary relay, a location attached to a name that appeared in the same procurement documentation. A verification contact: someone who had worked the contract audit, who had copies of the internal routing records, and who was willing to meet. Daniels had been mid-verification when Avril made the call. "I'm not done," Daniels had said. Not a protest. A statement of fact, the way he stated facts. "How long?" "Six hours. Maybe eight. There's a provenance gap in the contact's employment history I haven't been able to close. It might be nothing. It might not be." Avril had looked at the timeline. The contact had specified a window. The window was closing. He thought about CECOT. He thought about Louisville. He thought about how many times the correct call had been to move before the data was complete, because incomplete data was the permanent condition, and the window was the only thing that was real. "We go," he said. Daniels had looked at him. Not arguing — registering. The look of someone filing a fact about what had just happened and what it meant about the person who had decided it. "Yes," he said. He went back to his terminal. Reyes had taken the address. The room above a locksmith's shop in a city three hours away. He had arrived at the designated time and called back in four words: "Room's been cleared. Someone left something." The something was a single sheet of paper, folded once, on the floor near the door. Reyes had photographed it before touching it. Avril had read the photograph on his screen. It said: We know you were coming. He had sat with it for a long time. Daniels had come to stand beside him — not asked, just present, the way he was present when something required acknowledgment, and he didn't know yet what the acknowledgment should be. "The provenance gap in the contact's employment history," Daniels said. He said it quietly. Not told-you-so. Just the fact, returned to its context. "Yes," Avril said. Daniels had gone back to his terminal. He hadn't said anything else about it. He hadn't needed to. The verification contact was gone, and the internal routing records were gone, and the connection that would have closed the procurement chain at a specific level was gone, and they both knew why, and only one of them had made the call. Grey Sentinel may not have known the intelligence was compromised. The fragment may have been passed to him in good faith, already burned at the source. Or he had known and had decided the network needed to understand that its intelligence could be anticipated. Avril could not tell which. He had acted before he could tell, and that was the decision, and the decision had turned out to be wrong.

He thought about Lina Alvarez. He thought about her the way he always thought about her at moments like this — not as grief, not exactly, but as orientation. Twenty-seven. Civics teacher. Her name was called out as the van doors closed. He thought about the thing that had been true then and was still true: that the machine didn't distinguish between the immigration lawyer and the civics teacher and the data analyst and the mother standing in a courthouse holding a sign with her daughter's crayon on it. It used whatever designation was available. The category was whatever it needed to be. The outcome was the same.

The scarf was in his jacket pocket, as it always was. Cedar and ink, nearly gone now. He left it there.

He closed the Herrera file. He opened a new one.

Outside, Carrick was on the phone with the Sanctuary contact about SABLE_VERITY's route. Eliana was still in the back room — he could hear a low voice, a child's question, a low voice again. Mason had gone to sleep at the table with his head on his arms, which was something he did when the work had been long enough. The tea was cold.

The new file had no name yet. Just a verification code, a piece of paper, and two daughters whose father had decided that the testimony of people who processed chickens in Arkansas was worth the risk of his name ending up on a list.

He started writing things down.

Chapter Fifteen: Ripples

She had the shape of it by morning. Not the name — not yet — but the shape: a channel, a former program architect, a defection that had been in motion long enough that its traces were embedded in things that looked like noise until you knew what you were looking for.

The analyst who brought her the preliminary read had done good work. She told him so, which was not something she did casually. He understood what it meant and left without elaborating.

The rotation schedule had gone from one point to two hands. She could trace the first hand. The second was We Resist, which she already knew. What she needed was the channel between them, and the channel had a signature she recognized — not from current operations, but from a program she had signed off on eight years ago. A cognitive threat architect who had been cleared above the level of people who were supposed to know such things existed.

She understood, with the particular clarity that came from having spent a career in rooms where things were confirmed slowly and suspected quickly, that she had been working the wrong timeline. Not weeks. The defection had been years in the making. The documentation that had passed through that channel — the targeting list, the monitor-to-action mechanism, the Tower Sentinel records — had been assembled by someone who knew exactly what they were building and exactly who it was for.

She looked out at the city for a long time.

The question was not whether she could find the defector. She could find her. The question was what would be intact by the time she did.

Naomi Ellis had been awake before anyone else. Avril found her in the kitchen in the early gray, standing at the window with a cup of something that had gone cold, watching the street below with the particular vigilance of someone who had learned that the moment you stopped watching was the moment something moved.

She heard him come in and didn't turn. Anything on Carlos? she said.

Not yet, he said. We have people looking.

She nodded. The nod was the same one she'd given him in the van — acceptance of terms she hadn't chosen, offered without drama because drama cost something she was conserving. He had come to understand in the twenty hours since Louisville that Naomi Ellis was one of the most disciplined people he had ever been in a room with.

He knows we're out, she said. I keep telling myself that.

It's probably true.

Probably, she repeated. Not bitterly. Just precisely.

The older girl appeared in the doorway behind him — barefoot, hair still compressed from sleep, in an oversized shirt that had been found for her the night before. She looked at her mother. Her mother looked back. Something passed between them that had no words and didn't need them.

There's food, Avril said. Eliana put it together this morning.

The girl looked at him with the measured assessment of a child who had spent the last weeks deciding who could be trusted and on what evidence. Then she went to the table and sat down.

Naomi finally turned from the window. You should eat too, she said. You look like you haven't.

He hadn't. He sat down.

Mason found him after breakfast with the particular expression he used for things that were going to require adjustment.

She made it to the node, he said. Carrick confirmed at 0300. Clean transit, no flags on the route.

But, Avril said.

But the move burned her active channels—both of them. Mason set the tablet on the table. She's dark until she establishes new protocols from the node. That's not a quick process — she'll need to verify the node's integrity first, then build a new relay architecture from scratch. We're looking at days, not hours.

Avril absorbed that. Trina.

I called the dead drop this morning. She's been working through the treaty compliance files — she's made significant progress, she says the provenance chains are holding up to review. But the cross-reference she needs is on SABLE_VERITY's end of the documentation. The targeting list, the Tower Sentinel operational records. He paused. She can't complete the verification without them. And we can't reach SABLE_VERITY to get them.

The documentary convergence Daniels had named — the moment when Trina connected the treaty compliance files to Layer Nine and the whole architecture became a case instead of a collection of fragments — was sitting in a Sanctuary node with no active channel out. They had moved SABLE_VERITY to protect her and, in doing so, had, for the moment, protected the machine she was trying to help dismantle.

How long until she can establish new protocols, Avril asked.

If the node is clean and she's careful, four days minimum. Possibly a week.

Avril thought about the NSA Advisor and her directive and the shape of a search that was already narrowing. A week was a long time to be looking for someone and not find them. It was also a long time to be found.

Tell Trina to hold what she has and not contact us until we reach her, he said—no new channels. Everything stays cold until SABLE_VERITY is back.

Mason nodded. And the Herrera file?

Where's Daniels?

Daniels had been at the terminal since before dawn. He reported in the way he always did — standing, brief, with the flat precision of someone who had separated what he knew from what he suspected and was going to tell Avril only the first thing.

Tomás Herrera, he said. Immigration attorney, Little Rock, Arkansas. His practice specialized in undocumented agricultural workers — poultry processing plants, mainly, in a three-state region. In the fourteen months before his deportation, twelve of his clients filed workplace safety complaints with the state oversight board. Eight of those complaints referenced the same facility operator: a company called Regal Harvest LLC.

He set a printout on the table.

Regal Harvest LLC is a subsidiary of a holding company called Consolidated Agricultural Partners. Consolidated Agricultural Partners is one of four subsidiaries through which defence contractor Whitmore Group routes its domestic agricultural security contracts. He looked up. Whitmore Group appears in Grey Sentinel's treaty compliance files three times. It appears in the Layer Nine procurement architecture twice. It's the same company—different face.

Avril looked at the printout. The procurement chain ran from a poultry plant in Arkansas through four shell entities to a defence contractor that appeared in documentation going back to Tower Sentinel's current iteration.

Herrera's clients testified before the state board, Daniels continued. Two weeks later, Whitmore Group's agricultural security division flagged the plant as a site of potential labor organizing with national security implications under Emergency Enforcement Protocol B-12. Herrera was deported thirty-six hours after that flag was filed.

They had him disappear to protect a labor suppression contract, Avril said.

They disappeared him because he was pulling a thread that led somewhere they didn't want to be followed. Daniels picked the printout back up. Same as Carlos Ellis. Same as the people in the Tower Sentinel files. The designation changes. The mechanism doesn't.

Reyes had come in partway through and was leaning against the doorframe, listening. The family is in Honduras, he said. We don't have Sanctuary infrastructure there. We have a contact in the region, but we haven't used them in two years, and I wouldn't trust that channel without fresh verification.

I know, Avril said. That's not a decision for today. Today it's information.

He looked at the printout for a moment longer. Whitmore Group. Four subsidiaries. A poultry plant in Arkansas, a deportation order, and two children whose father had thought that testimony mattered.

He thought about what Carrick had said the night before: It's not random.

It wasn't.

The message arrived through the established relay — the dead-drop architecture that Grey Sentinel had used since the Geneva meeting, verified at each node by the protocol they had agreed on in the municipal archive. Avril read it at the table with Daniels still present, which he would have preferred to avoid and couldn't, given the timing.

FROM: GREY SENTINEL

RELAY: ECHO-NINE / THREE NODES

MESSAGE: You've drawn attention you may not have clocked. NGC-Protec ran drone drift analysis over the Louisville corridor beginning forty-eight hours before your op. Not reactive — pre-positioned. Someone filed a coverage request before the transfer was publicly scheduled. That means foreknowledge of the transfer, which means the off-book contract was leaking at the contracting level. The same entity that filed the NGC-Protec coverage request appears in procurement records connected to Whitmore Group. I'm sending the cross-reference separately. Use your own judgment about what it means that they were watching before you were.

One question, when you have time: who else knew about the rotation schedule besides the source you moved?

Avril read it twice. Then he looked at Daniels.

Daniels was already thinking about it — he had the particular stillness of someone whose mind was running faster than his face. NGC-Protec and Whitmore Group are in the same procurement thread, he said. That's not coincidence. That's infrastructure. They're not just watching the operations — they're integrated into the contracting chain that creates the conditions the operations respond to.

They fund the detention, Avril said. And then they watch for anyone who tries to undo it.

And bill for both, Daniels said. It was the driest thing he had ever said. Avril almost didn't catch it.

He looked at the last line of Grey Sentinel's message again. Who else knew about the rotation schedule besides the source you moved? It was a precise question. It wasn't asking whether the source had been compromised — it was asking whether the leak was the source or the channel. Whether the problem was SABLE_VERITY or the relay she'd used to send the schedule.

Those were different problems. Significantly different.

I need Carrick, Avril said.

Carrick listened to all of it without interrupting — Grey Sentinel's question, the NGC-Protec pre-positioning, the Whitmore Group thread, the relay architecture SABLE_VERITY had used to send the rotation schedule. When Avril finished, Carrick was quiet for a long moment.

The relay she used was a dead channel, he said finally. Dormant for six months before she reactivated it for the schedule. If someone was watching that channel, they were watching it before she used it. A pause. Which means they weren't watching her. They were watching the channel.

Someone who knew the channel existed, Avril said.

Someone who knew it well enough to know it would be used for something worth watching. Carrick looked at the floor for a moment. That's a short list.

Yes.

Neither of them said what the short list implied — that the channel's provenance ran back through the same apparatus SABLE_VERITY had spent years inside, and that the person watching it might not be the NSA Advisor's office at all. Might be something older. Something that had been watching long before SABLE_VERITY decided to walk out.

They left it there for now. Some things needed to sit before they could be looked at directly.

Later, alone, Avril sat with the Herrera file and Grey Sentinel's message and the knowledge that SABLE_VERITY was dark somewhere in a Sanctuary node with documentation that the world needed and couldn't currently reach. Naomi Ellis was asleep in the back room with her children. Carlos was in a facility whose location Reyes was still trying to confirm. Trina Cole was holding still with half a verification complete. The Whitmore Group thread ran from a poultry plant in Arkansas to a defence contractor to a procurement chain that had been operating for at least as long as Tower Sentinel, which was at least as long as Lina Alvarez had been gone.

He opened Grey Sentinel's message again and read the last line.

Who else knew about the rotation schedule besides the source you moved?

He didn't have an answer yet. He understood that finding one was now the most important thing he could do, and that it was going to require looking at someone he trusted in a way he didn't want to look at them. He opened the SHADOW document. The Mason entries were there: the deprecated server ping, the briefing summary that had circulated with a detail that shouldn't have been in it. Two entries. Both thin. Both explainable. Both still there. He made a decision. He drafted a message — not a real communication, a test. A fragment of operational detail about a meeting that didn't exist, routed through a relay that would show him whether the information moved and where it moved to. He sent it to Mason only. He told no one else. Then he waited. Forty-six hours later, the fragment hadn't moved. Daniels' monitoring showed nothing — no lateral transmission, no echo on any channel they were watching, no sign the information had gone anywhere except wherever Mason stored things he'd been told. Avril ran the check twice. He ran it a third time at two in the morning, sitting alone at the table with the city making its quiet sounds outside. Nothing. He sat with it for a long time. Then he opened the SHADOW document and deleted the Mason entries — both of them, the server ping and the briefing detail, gone, the document shorter by two lines. He didn't add a note explaining the deletion. He just removed them. The feeling that followed was not relief exactly. It was the specific uncomfortable weight of having been wrong about someone he'd been watching carefully, and knowing that the watching had been necessary, and knowing that the person he'd been watching had no idea it had happened and never would. He had suspected Mason. He had tested him. Mason had come back clean. None of this was something he could explain or apologize for, because explaining it would require admitting it, and admitting it would do damage he wasn't willing to do. He added one line to a different part of the SHADOW document — not about Mason, but about the test itself, what he'd learned about the channel. What the absence of movement told him about where the leak was and wasn't. The wrong accusation had produced real information, which was its own kind of uncomfortable. He left the question open. He started writing.

Chapter Sixteen: Interference

The channel had a history. That was what the analyst had brought her at seven in the morning, and it was the thing that changed the shape of everything she thought she knew about the timeline.

The relay architecture SABLE_VERITY had used to transmit the rotation schedule was not new. It had been built, she could see now, tracing it backward through infrastructure logs that required three separate clearance levels to access, during a period when SABLE_VERITY was still an active agency asset. Not a dead channel reactivated. A channel she had built herself, years ago, and left dormant until she needed it.

Which meant it had been inside the apparatus the entire time. Which meant that anyone with access to the apparatus's legacy infrastructure logs could have been watching it for years.

She looked at the analyst. "How many people have clearance to those logs?"

He told her. The number was small. She already knew most of the names.

She sent him out and sat alone for a while, looking at the city. She had spent years assuming the problem was external, a defector, a leak, a civilian archivist assembling something from outside. She was beginning to understand that the channel's history made the problem much older and much closer than that.

She was one step from the name. She was not certain, yet, that she wanted to take it.

Mason brought it mid-morning, with the particular expression he reserved for news that was better than expected but came with a condition attached.

"She's back," he said. "New protocols established by the node. Contact re-established as of 0600."

Avril looked up from the Herrera file. "Clean?"

"She says so. But she included something." He set the tablet on the table. "She knows the channel was being watched. She found a passive listener embedded in the relay architecture, dormant, no active collection, just a flag that would trip if the channel was used. She says she should have checked before she used it."

"She didn't know it was there," Avril said.

"She built the channel," Mason said. "She says that's exactly why she should have known."

The weight of that sat for a moment. SABLE_VERITY had built the relay herself, years ago, inside the apparatus. The passive listener had been placed by someone who knew the channel existed and understood that she might eventually use it. Not to collect, to be notified.

"Who placed the listener?" Avril asked.

"She doesn't know. She found the flag, not the origin. It's older than her defection, she thinks it predates her decision to leave by at least two years." Mason paused. "Which means someone was watching the channel before she decided to use it. Before she decided to come to us."

Grey Sentinel's question from Chapter 14 was in the room without being spoken: "Who else knew about the rotation schedule besides the source you moved?" The answer was beginning to have a shape, and the shape was not SABLE_VERITY.

"Get Carrick," Avril said. "And tell Trina she can resume. Tell her to move carefully, the documentation she's reviewing connects to people who are now looking very hard at everything connected to it."

Mason nodded. "One more thing. She, SABLE_VERITY, asked me to tell you that the targeting list and the Tower Sentinel operational records are intact. She's ready to transfer them through the new protocols when you give the word."

"Not yet," Avril said. "When Trina's ready for them. Not before."

Reyes had found it through a cross-reference he had been running for six days, transfer manifests from three separate federal logistics contractors, triangulated against a pattern of unscheduled supply deliveries to a location in western Tennessee that had no public-facing operational record. A former agricultural processing facility outside Waverly, repurposed under a lease arrangement that ran through one of the four subsidiaries Daniels had identified in the Whitmore Group chain.

He told Avril first, then asked whether he should be the one to tell Naomi.

Avril thought about it. "Yes," he said. "You found it. That matters."

He stood in the doorway of the back room while Reyes did it, not listening to the words but watching Naomi's face. She absorbed the information the way she absorbed everything, without the collapse of composure that fear produced in people who had not been living with fear for months. Her jaw shifted. Her hands, folded in her lap, tightened once and then released.

When Reyes finished, she said, "Is he okay?"

"We don't have eyes inside," Reyes said. "We have a location. That's what we have right now."

She nodded. The nod was the same one she had given Avril in the van, in the corridor outside the kitchen, in every moment since Louisville, where the answer had been not yet rather than yes. She had become, over the days in the safehouse, someone Avril thought about when he thought about what the work was actually for, not the machinery of it, the documentation and the procurement chains and the surveillance architecture, but the person sitting in a chair in a back room who had decided that composure was the thing she could still control.

The older girl was at the table in the corner with a book Eliana had found for her. She was reading it, or appeared to be. Avril suspected she had heard everything.

He left them there and went to find Carrick.

Mason had been watching the disinformation pattern for two days before he brought it. That was characteristic. He collected until he had enough to say something useful, then said it once and left the implications to settle.

"Coordinated campaign," he said. "Started about seventy-two hours ago. Multiple platforms, multiple origin points, two of which trace back to domestic troll infrastructure and one to an Estonian commercial IP cluster that's been associated with contract disinfo work for state-adjacent clients." He set his laptop open on the table. "The content is a mix, repurposed protest footage with altered signage, a federal spokesperson statement that's been selectively cut, and this."

He played the video without commentary.

It was forty seconds. Nighttime footage, grainy, a rooftop angle on a street-level scene. Three figures in dark clothing were approaching a building. The camera held on the middle figure as he turned slightly, not a full face reveal, just enough. The frame, the gait, the angle of the shoulders. And at the edge of his jacket collar, catching the available light for a single second before he moved out of frame, a length of gray wool.

Avril watched it once. Then he looked at the table for a moment.

"They know about the scarf," he said. It came out flat, which was how things came out when they were significant enough that tone felt insufficient.

"They've been watching long enough to clock it," Mason said. "That video was constructed. The gait analysis, the frame matching, that's not a coincidence of footage. Someone assembled it deliberately."

"From what source material?"

"At least two verified public appearances from early in the network's history, before we tightened protocols. Plus something more recent, the angle suggests a camera position we haven't identified yet." He paused. "The scarf is the tell. It's not visible in the public footage. It had to come from closer in."

Eliana, who had come in from the kitchen, had been standing at the edge of the room since the video started. She did not say anything for a moment. Then: "The deepfake is the least of it. If they have a camera position we haven't found, the question is what else they've collected from it."

"Yes," Mason said. "It is."

Carrick was already thinking about the room's entry points. Avril could tell by the way he was standing.

The attachment Grey Sentinel had sent with his message two days earlier had taken Daniels that long to work through fully. He reported in the afternoon, after Carrick had finished his sweep of the safehouse's exterior positions, after Mason had sent the counter-surveillance protocol to the node operators, after the particular business of a day that had already been too full had begun to settle.

He set a printout on the table. Three fragments, the rest redacted or missing. He had flagged the ones that mattered.

The first read: ENTITY: CIVILIAN-ORIGIN ASYMMETRIC ORGANIZATION. STATUS: ELEVATED THREAT POTENTIAL, TIER 3A. AUTHORIZED: BEHAVIORAL PROFILING VIA SIGINT FUSION. AI PATTERN MODELING, ACTIVE, FREQUENCY ANALYSIS, DEVICE TRIANGULATION, BEHAVIORAL DRIFT.

"Behavioral drift," Daniels said. "It means they're not trying to break our encryption. They're modeling our decision patterns. Who talks to whom, in what sequence, before an operation? What changes in communication behavior in the forty-eight hours before we move? They train the model on historical data and use it to predict the future."

"They're not listening to what we say," Carrick said. "They're learning to guess what we'll do."

"Correct." Daniels turned to the second fragment: COORDINATION: FRIENDLY NATION PARTNERS FOR EXTRADITION FALLBACK. IDENTIFICATION OF HIGH-VALUE LEADERSHIP NODES.

Nobody said anything about what came after identification.

The third fragment was the last one and the shortest: BEHAVIORAL INDICATORS SUGGEST PRIMARY NODE OPERATES UNDER HIGH-MORAL EQUILIBRIUM BIAS. RECOMMEND PSYCHOLOGICAL PRESSURE SCENARIOS TO DESTABILIZE ALIGNMENT.

Reyes read it twice. "They think they can break your judgment," he said to Avril. "Put you in situations where the moral calculus is impossible and wait for you to make a mistake."

"They've been doing that," Eliana said quietly. "Every impossible case that arrives. Every family that can't wait. Every thread that pulls in a different direction from the one you're already following." She looked at the fragment. "They may not have engineered all of it. But they understand how to exploit it."

The room held that for a long moment.

"Counter-behavior," Daniels said, eventually. "We vary patterns. No reuse of communication sequences. We introduce noise into the behavioral signature, decisions that don't follow from precedent, and communication rhythms that don't cluster. We make the model's training data unreliable."

"How long does that take?" Avril asked.

"To degrade a model that's had months of good data?" Daniels considered it. "Weeks of consistent noise. Maybe longer."

"Then we start tonight," Avril said.

Late. The safehouse had the quality it always had at this hour, the particular density of a space where too many things were unresolved and the people responsible for resolving them had temporarily run out of day.

Carrick was outside doing a final perimeter check. Reyes was at the terminal running the counter-behavior protocol Daniels had drafted. Mason had found the unidentified camera position, or thought he had, a disused ventilation housing across the street that would have had a sightline to the building's main entrance for approximately six months before a scaffolding project had blocked it. He had documented it and gone to bed.

Eliana was still awake. He could see the light under the library door.

Avril sat at the table with the three directive fragments in front of him and the deepfake still running somewhere in his memory, the gray wool at the edge of the figure's collar, lit for one second by whatever ambient light existed on that constructed rooftop. They had built the figure carefully enough to include a detail that no public footage contained. That required time, proximity, and the particular patience of surveillance.

He took the scarf out of his jacket pocket. It had been there so long, the shape of it had conformed to the pocket, an object that had stopped being a choice and become a habit. Cedar and ink, nearly gone. The smell you had to want to find.

He thought about Lena, where she was, whether she was safe and whether moving had been enough. Whether two years of silence had been protection or just absence, and whether she had noticed the difference.

His secondary device vibrated once on the table. The We Resist inbox, not the operational channel. He picked it up.

The address was one he did not recognize. The message was four sentences. He read the first one, and his body understood before his mind did, the phrasing, the particular cadence, the specific detail in the third sentence that no one else would have known to include. Something she had said to him once, years ago, that had become a kind of private shorthand. She had been watching. She had found a channel. She was afraid.

He sat with it for a long time. Forty seconds, maybe.

Long enough to know what the correct decision was. Long enough to understand that he was not going to make it.

He typed one line. He did not think about what it said. His hands moved before his judgment could catch up, which was the point of the trap, which was what made it not a trap but something worse, a reflex. The kind of thing you did because you were still a person, and persons responded when the people they loved reached out from the dark.

He sent it. He put the device face down on the table. He sat there for a moment with his hands flat on the surface, looking at the wall.

He did not know if she would see it. He did not know if it was already too late for it to matter, or if the damage had been done the moment her message reached him, or if nothing had happened yet and he had just made it happen.

He did not know. He would not know for weeks. And when he found out, the knowing would be a specific kind of knowledge, the kind that arrived after the fact, when there was nothing left to do with it except carry it.

He picked up the device. He deleted the exchange from the inbox. He did not tell anyone.

He thought about Naomi in the back room, the older girl reading, the not-yet that was all he had been able to give them. He thought about Carlos in a repurposed agricultural facility in western Tennessee, and whether knowing where he was made things better or only made the distance more precise.

He thought about Lina Alvarez. Twenty-seven. Civics teacher. The van doors. He thought about how the machine now knew enough about him to build a version of him, his gait, his frame, his scarf, and use it to make him into the thing they needed him to be in the story they were writing. He thought about how that was not new. The machine had always been writing the story. The work, from the beginning, had been to write a different one.

He folded the scarf and put it back.

He opened the counter-behavior protocol and began working through it. It was going to be a long night, and the night had its own requirements, and he would meet them the same way he had met every other requirement since this began, one decision at a time, with the knowledge that the decisions were the only thing he actually controlled.

In the back room, one of the children was breathing in a careful, deliberate way. He could hear it through the wall. It was steady.

He kept working.

Chapter Seventeen: Inside Voices

The room was not on the building's floor plan. She knew this because she had checked twice, in the weeks since she had begun to understand that the problem she was working on was not the problem she had been assigned. The floor plan was one of many documents that told a partial truth, and she had learned to prefer partial truths to complete ones, because a complete truth required a name at the end of it.

There were two other people in the room. She did not name them here, even in her own thinking, because names had become liabilities and she was still deciding whose liabilities were whose.

The first wanted to move. Had wanted to move for months, in the way that people wanted to move when they had run out of patience for the complexity of the situation they were in, and had decided that the cost of action was lower than the cost of continued thinking. He used the word "insurgency." He used it with the confidence of someone who had made the word do a great deal of work in the past and expected it to work again.

The second was quieter. Younger than either of them. He had the particular quality of someone who had been in rooms where words led directly to outcomes and had learned to listen very carefully before adding to the vocabulary of a room. He said, "They're ghosts that save people." He said it as a tactical observation, not a compliment. He was right that it was a tactical problem.

She listened to both of them. She had been doing this for years, the skill of appearing to be deciding when she was actually learning. What she was learning, in this room, on this morning, was that neither of the people she was sitting with knew what she knew about the channel. Neither of them knew about the listener that had been placed before the defection. Neither of them knew that the problem she was working on was not a civilian archivist with operational ambitions.

The problem she was working on was something that had been running for years inside the apparatus itself, and that she was now one of a very small number of people positioned to see it.

The first voice said, "When they force our hand, we will break theirs."

She said nothing. She was thinking about the channel. About the name. She had not thought about what it would mean to take it and what it would mean not to.

After the room emptied, she sat alone for a while and looked at the partial truths on the table in front of her. Then she picked up the phone.

Not to act. To listen. There was still a difference.

Naomi's older daughter had found a routine. Eliana had engineered it, the way she engineered most things that mattered in the safehouse, without announcing it, by making the materials available and waiting. There was a battered world atlas on the shelf. The girl had been working through it for three days now, a page at a time, writing the names of capitals in a small notebook she had been given. Not asked to do it. Just doing it.

Avril watched this for a moment when he came through in the morning and then moved on, because looking at it too long cost something he needed for other things.

Naomi was at the table with Mason. They were not talking. He was working, and she was drinking coffee, and the silence between them was the functional kind that people found when they had been in the same space long enough that the presence of another person stopped requiring management. Avril thought this was one of Mason's understated skills and that it was probably not accidental.

"Grey Sentinel," Mason said, without looking up. "The message came through the relay overnight. He flagged it as unusual and passed it on without a read."

"Without a read," Avril said.

"His word was 'clean.' Channel provenance is clean. He doesn't know who sent it. He's not making a recommendation." Mason set the tablet on the table. "He said to tell you he's been watching that channel for eleven months and nothing has ever come through it."

Avril looked at Naomi. She was not looking at him. She was looking at her coffee with the focused attention of someone who had decided that the conversation happening near her was not hers to be part of.

He took the tablet and went into the other room.

The message was forty-three words. No headers. No signature. No channel markers beyond what Grey Sentinel had already stripped.

OUR SYSTEM HAS NOT FAILED. IT HAS BEEN CAPTURED. NOT EVERYONE INSIDE IT AGREES. SOME OF US STILL BELIEVE IN A CONSTITUTIONAL BALANCE OF POWERS. IF YOU ARE WILLING TO TALK, THERE IS A DOOR. NO COMMITMENTS. JUST A VOICE ACROSS THE GAP. YOU ARE NOT ALONE.

He read it three times. Not because it was ambiguous. It was very clear, which was what made it worth reading three times. Someone who could use a channel that Grey Sentinel's network had been watching for eleven months without a single transmission, and who knew it, had decided that now was the moment to use it.

That was nothing.

He brought it to Carrick first, which was where he brought things that were potentially dangerous and required an honest assessment of danger rather than a hopeful one.

Carrick read it once. "It's a channel Grey Sentinel trusts. That's nothing. It's also not enough." He set the tablet down. "Someone inside the apparatus wants a conversation. Best case, it's what it says, a faction that's been watching and decided watching isn't enough. Worst case, they've done their homework, they know how Grey Sentinel operates, and they built a credential specifically to get through this door."

"How would they know about that channel?" Avril said.

"Same way they knew about the rotation schedule," Carrick said. "In the same way, someone knew the CSI-7 transfer window." He did not say more. He did not need to.

Avril brought it to Eliana. She read it standing, the way she read things she was going to say something careful about.

"The cost of not listening," she said, "is that we stay in a sealed room while the building around us changes." She handed the tablet back. "I'm not saying trust it. I'm saying the information it could carry, if it's real, is the kind we can't build from outside. We've been trying to document the architecture for months. Someone who was inside it, who wants to talk, who knows which door to knock on..." She stopped. "That's the kind of source that changes what's possible."

Reyes, from the doorway, said, "One condition. We don't meet them. Not yet. We ask a question first, something only someone genuinely inside would know. If they answer it correctly, we consider the next steps. If they don't, we burn the channel and move."

The room settled into the particular quiet that followed a decision, finding its shape.

"I'll send it," Avril said. "Tonight. One question. No identifiers."

He looked at the forty-three words again. Someone on the other side of a door that Grey Sentinel had been watching for eleven months. Waiting to see if anyone would knock back.

He had been running the CSI-7 timing logs intermittently for two weeks, not because he had a specific suspicion but because Grey Sentinel's question from Chapter 14, "Who else knew about the rotation schedule besides the source you moved?" had never closed. SABLE_VERITY's disclosure of the passive listener had answered part of it. The part it had not answered was forward-facing: if the listener had been placed by someone who knew the channel, and if that someone was not the NSA Advisor's office, then there was a third party who had known about the CSI-7 operation before it happened.

He had been looking for evidence of that third party in the data they had generated themselves.

Tonight, he found something.

It was in the transfer window authorization, the timestamp sequence that logged when the team's entry protocol synchronized with SABLE_VERITY's guard rotation data. The sequence was correct. The timing was correct. But there was a lag of eleven seconds between the authorization request and the confirmation, in a handshake that should have taken three.

Eleven seconds was not a transmission delay. Eleven seconds was a read.

Someone had received the authorization request, read it, and then passed it through. Not intercepted it. The data was intact, the sequence unbroken. Passed it through like a hand opening a door and closing it again so quietly that the person walking through did not notice.

He ran it twice more. The lag was consistent across both redundant logs. It had not been in the pre-op dry run.

He opened the worn notebook. He wrote three things:

CSI-7 auth lag: 11 sec. Pre-op: 3 sec. Not transmission.

Appeared between the authorization request and confirmation.

Consistent across both logs. Not present in the dry run.

He did not write an interpretation. He had learned, over the months of building this file, that interpretation was what you did after you had more than three facts, and he had three facts. He closed the notebook.

He sat for a while in the dark, the laptop closed, the room quiet. From the back, the slow, steady breathing of the older girl. She had moved the atlas to her mattress and fallen asleep with it open on the page for the countries of Central America. He could see the corner of it from where he sat.

He thought about who had known the transfer window. SABLE_VERITY. Mason. Carrick. Reyes. Eliana. Himself.

He thought about what it meant that all of those people had been in the same room.

He did not take the scarf out of his pocket. He thought about Lina Alvarez instead. Twenty-seven, a civics teacher, the twenty-three seconds, the van doors. The way he always thought about her when the problem he was working on got close enough to the bone that the technical details stopped being sufficient. The machine that had taken her had been running for a long time before anyone knew to look back. The passive listener had been placed two years before SABLE_VERITY's defection. The transfer window lag was consistent across both logs.

The machine had been inside before he built the thing that was supposed to be outside it.

He opened the notebook again and wrote a fourth fact:

All people with transfer window knowledge were present when the channel was established.

He closed it. He sat with it. Not the technical implication. That was clear, and clarity was not the problem. The problem was what the technical implication meant about the room itself. The people in it. The trust he had built, carefully, over months of watching each of them under pressure and deciding they held. He had been right about that. He was probably still right about that. The lag of eleven seconds did not name a person. It was named a moment, a hand on a door, a decision, a read. He did not know whose hand. He understood that finding out would require him to look directly at people he had decided to trust, and that the decision to trust them had not been wrong, and that neither of those things cancelled the other.

He did not sleep, but the quality of the wakefulness was different from how it had been. It was the specific alertness of someone who had found the beginning of a thread and was deciding whether to pull it.

He left it there. For tonight, the thread was enough.

Chapter Eighteen: The Third Branch

"Two signals." She had been carrying both of them for four days now, turning them over in the way you turned over a thing when you could not yet see whether it was one thing or two.

The first: the channel provenance. She had traced it as far as it could be traced without taking the final step, the step that would produce a name, and the name would require a decision, and she was still deciding whether she wanted to make that decision inside the current structure or outside it. Some decisions, she had learned, became irreversible the moment you moved them from private to institutional. She was being careful about which category this one belonged to.

The second: someone from inside the program had made contact with the civilian network. She knew this because the program had left traces, the kind of traces that only someone who had been very close to its operational core would know to leave. The traces did not tell her who. They told her the person knew how things worked. That was its own kind of credential, and also its own kind of danger.

What she did not know was whether the two signals were the same problem. She had begun to suspect they were. She was not yet ready to confirm it.

She went back to the channel provenance. She looked at the name she had not taken yet. She put it down again.

Not yet. But soon.

Grey Sentinel's response came through the relay two days after Avril had sent the question. The answer had come back in three parts. The first two were correct, specific, verifiable, the kind of knowledge that required either genuine access or a very elaborate construction. The third was partial: the contact had answered the factual question but left one element unverified, in a way that suggested either caution or incomplete knowledge. Avril could not tell which.

He told Mason to flag it as an incomplete pass rather than confirmed, and then he sat with that for a day before deciding what to do with it.

What he did was reply. One line: If you want to meet, choose the location. We will not choose it for you.

The location had come back within six hours. A seminary in upstate New York, on a Tuesday, at a time. Grey Sentinel had added a single word to the relay: Clean. No recommendation. The second time, he had passed something through without a recommendation, which Avril had begun to understand as Grey Sentinel's version of a very strong one.

He told Carrick before he told anyone else.

"An incomplete pass means they either did not know the full answer or did not want to show all of it yet," Carrick said. "Could be caution. Could be they are building a credential incrementally, so you cannot verify it all at once."

"Yes," Avril said.

"You are going anyway."

"Grey Sentinel thinks the channel is clean. I trust Grey Sentinel's judgment on channels."

"That is not the same as trusting the person using the channel."

"No," Avril said. "It is not."

Carrick looked at him for a moment. "I will be outside," he said, "out of sight. If it turns, make noise."

The building had been a seminary for forty years, a storage facility for twenty, and nothing for the last six. The cold had worked its way into the stone in the manner of cold in old buildings, not a draft but a presence, patient and total. The chapel still had its windows. The light through them was the particular flat gray of a November afternoon in upstate New York.

The scarf was on because it was cold and because he had stopped some time ago pretending it was a choice. Cedar and ink, nearly gone. He barely noticed the smell now. He noticed the weight.

The man was already there when Avril arrived. Sixties, gray coat, the careful posture of someone who had spent years in rooms where being noticed was a professional liability. He put nothing on the table. He did not extend a hand.

"You sent an incomplete answer," Avril said.

"I sent you everything I knew with certainty," the man said. "The rest I suspected. I did not want to give you a confident answer to a question I was not sure about."

Avril looked at him. It was a reasonable thing to say. It was also exactly what someone constructing a credential would say. He filed both possibilities and moved on.

"You know things about the program's architecture," Avril said. "The question I sent required access at a level that very few people had. Tell me how you had it."

"I was inside a different part of it," the man said. "Not the operational side. The oversight side, what passed for oversight. I was one of four people who reviewed the targeting criteria documentation before it was classified at the level that made review impossible. I saw what the criteria were. I saw what they were designed to produce. And I wrote an objection that no one read because by the time I wrote it, the channel for objections had been reclassified away from me."

He reached into the inside pocket of his coat and placed a single document on the table. No folder. Just a page, creased from being carried.

"I have been holding this for three years," he said. "Waiting for a moment when giving it to someone would mean something. I think this is that moment."

Avril picked it up. It was a summary, two paragraphs, bureaucratic language, dated three years earlier. The targeting criteria for a domestic surveillance program were described in a review document. The criteria included: association with immigration advocacy organizations, contact with journalists covering immigration enforcement, and provision of legal services to undocumented individuals.

He read it twice. He read it the second time carefully, because the first time he had felt something he needed to set aside before he could read it properly.

"There is a woman," the man said. "A systems analyst. She documented the program's implementation, not the criteria, the actual targeting lists and the specific individuals flagged. She took it through every proper channel. Inspector general. Legal counsel. Congressional inquiry. A district court ordered her released two weeks ago. The order is on paper and nowhere else."

"Where is she?" Avril said.

"Private facility in eastern Pennsylvania. It operates under a corporate lease. The leaseholder is a subsidiary of."

"Whitmore Group," Avril said.

The man stopped. He looked at Avril with the particular attention of someone recalibrating. "You know the name."

"I know the architecture," Avril said. He kept his face still. He was thinking about Tomás Herrera and Carlos Ellis and the procurement chain that Daniels had traced, and he was thinking about the targeting criteria on the page in his hand, association with immigration advocacy organizations, and the particular precision with which the machine had been using that criterion to remove people who knew too much about its own operation.

The whistleblower had not disclosed a surveillance program. She had disclosed the mechanism by which the machine protected itself from the people who might expose it.

He did not say this aloud. He folded the document and put it in his jacket, next to the scarf.

"Does she know what she found?" he asked.

"She knows what she documented," the man said. "Whether she understands the full scope, I do not know. I am not sure I understand the full scope."

"What do you want from us?" Avril said.

"I want the court order enforced," he said. "I want her out of that facility. I do not need credit. I do not need a record. I need the thing the court ordered to actually happen."

A long silence. The flat gray light. The cold that had been in the stone for years.

"I will need to talk to my team," Avril said.

The man nodded. "I know. I am not asking for an answer today." He picked up his coat from the pew beside him. "I am asking you to understand what she found, and to decide whether that matters enough."

He left without looking back. His footsteps echoed in the stone until they did not.

Avril sat in the cold chapel for a while with the document in his jacket and the scarf around his neck and the flat gray light coming through the old windows. He thought about the targeting criteria. He thought about what it meant to be flagged for providing legal services to undocumented individuals.

He went to find Carrick.

The document went around the table once. Nobody said anything while they were reading it, which was the right response.

Naomi Ellis was at the table. She had not been asked to leave, and no one had suggested it, which Avril had decided was the correct call. She had been in the building for weeks. She understood the register of these conversations. Her presence was a fact the team worked around rather than a problem it solved. She read the targeting criteria the way she had read everything since Louisville, without losing composure, with the particular economy of someone who already knew things like this existed and was simply watching the documentation catch up.

"Private facility, eastern Pennsylvania," Reyes said. "Whitmore Group is the leaseholder. If it is the same contracting structure as

CSI-7 and Waverly, we can cross-reference the procurement chain. It will take Daniels a day, maybe two."

"Do it," Avril said.

Carrick had been standing near the window. "Incomplete pass on the credential," he said. "We do not know what he did not tell you, or why."

"No," Avril said. "We do not."

"The channel was clean," Eliana said. "Grey Sentinel's word. And the document is real, the format, the classification markings, the date. I have seen enough of this kind of paperwork to know what fabrication looks like. This is not fabricated."

"The document being real does not make the contact trustworthy," Carrick said.

"No," Eliana said. "But a real document held for three years, passed to us through a channel Grey Sentinel has been watching for eleven months, that is a cost. Someone paid it." She paused. "The woman in that facility paid a different cost. And she paid it through every proper channel available to her before those channels were closed."

The room was quiet for a moment.

"The ghost print," Avril said, looking at Daniels. "If we run an op, I want you on the timing logs. Not the external surveillance, the internal sequence. Same methodology as the CSI-7 audit. If the signature fires, I want a timestamp."

Daniels looked at him steadily. He understood exactly what was being asked and what it meant for the short list of people who had known the CSI-7 transfer window. "Yes," he said.

That was all. The room absorbed it.

"Thirty-six hours to confirm the procurement chain," Reyes said. "If it traces back to Whitmore Group, we know the facility structure. If it does not, we reassess."

"Agreed," Avril said.

Mason had been at the terminal since Avril came back from the seminary. He turned now. "SABLE_VERITY flagged something this morning. She says the targeting criteria document, if it is the one she thinks it is, is the upstream record for the domestic targeting list she has been holding. The one she said would fill in what the treaty compliance files do not show." He paused. "She says Trina needs to see it."

The room was very still.

"Send her a copy through the verified channel," Avril said. "Tell SABLE_VERITY to hold the list until Trina confirms she has the criteria document and is ready to cross-reference."

He looked at the document one more time, two paragraphs, bureaucratic language, three years old. The upstream record for everything they had been building toward. Sitting in a jacket pocket next to a nearly spent scarf.

He thought about how long the machine had been running before any of them knew to look. He thought about the woman in the facility in eastern Pennsylvania, who had found the document at its source and tried to hand it to the people whose job it was to care, and had ended up in a building whose address did not exist on any public record.

He closed the file.

"We go in thirty-six hours," he said. "Reyes leads logistics. Carrick leads the entry. Eliana is on the outside. Soto drives. Daniels handles internal surveillance." He looked around the room. "We do not move until Reyes confirms the procurement chain. If the structure is what we think it is, we know how the facility operates. If it is not, we stop."

Nobody objected.

Naomi Ellis was still at the table. She had not said anything throughout. But when Avril stood up, she looked at him with the expression of someone who had been sitting in a room full of people deciding to do something difficult and had decided, quietly, that this was what it looked like when people tried.

He did not say anything to her. He did not need to.

Chapter Nineteen: The Extraction

She had taken the name the night before.

Not formally. Not through a channel that would create a record. She had written it on paper, looked at it for a long time, and then burned the paper, which meant the name existed only in the one place she could not burn. She had been carrying it since then with the particular weight of something that had stopped being a question and become a decision she had not yet acted on.

The decision had a shape: she could move through the institution with it, let it become a directive, watch it travel through the apparatus toward consequences she could anticipate but not fully control. Or she could hold it outside the institution, carry it alone, decide what it meant to know this specific thing without the institution knowing she knew it.

She had spent her career inside the institution. She understood its logic, its reach, and its tendency to make individual judgment impossible by distributing it across too many layers to be traceable. She also understood that the problem she was now holding had been produced by that same tendency.

The name was not a traitor's name. It was a witness's name. That distinction had taken her a long time to see clearly, and she was still deciding what it had changed.

She put the paper in her coat pocket. She went to work.

Reyes had confirmed the procurement chain thirty-one hours earlier. The facility leaseholder traced to a subsidiary of Consolidated Agricultural Partners, Whitmore Group, the fourth entity in the chain, with the same structure as CSI-7 and Waverly. They knew how the facility operated. They knew which layers of the contracting structure handled security. They knew, from two previous ops, where the gaps were likely to be.

It was Carrick who said it was enough to move. He said it without ceremony, which was how he said things that were decisions rather than opinions.

They went in at first light. Cold morning, the kind of cold that had been in the air for days and had settled into things, the ground, the equipment, the collar of the jacket Avril wore over the maintenance uniform. The scarf was underneath, against his neck. He had stopped registering it as a choice.

Soto drove. Eliana held the exterior line. She had the same quality of stillness at a facility perimeter that she had in a courtroom, reading what was happening without appearing to be reading it. Reyes had planted the identity packet three weeks earlier through a shell entity that had never done anything suspicious and would never do anything again. Carrick led. Avril was behind him. The cases between them held equipment that was what it claimed to be, and also other things.

The gate buzzer. The voice. "Team 3. You're early."

"Clock's ticking," Avril said. "Fiber integrity check. Network pulse dropped below baseline last night."

A pause. "Gate 2. South hall. Sign in with Reyes."

The gate opened. They moved without hurry, which was the only way to move through a facility that was waiting for someone to hurry.

The interior was colder than the outside, which Avril had noted at CSI-7 and Waverly, too; climate control was calibrated to a specific kind of discomfort, the kind that made people want to finish their business and leave. The security presence was light: one armed guard at the secondary checkpoint who waved them through when Reyes's work order passed the scanner. The hallways branched in ways the floor plan had predicted. They moved through them the way you moved through something you had memorized, not hesitating, not consulting.

Daniels was on the internal surveillance channel. Not comms, a silent monitoring thread that would log sequence anomalies against the baseline Avril had established from the CSI-7 and rotation schedule timing data. If the ghost print fired, Daniels would see it. He would say nothing on comms. He would record the timestamp.

They reached the central node junction. Avril pulled the tablet and entered the root command. The signal patch went live.

"Nine minutes of baseline silence," Daniels said in his ear. "Holding block two left turns. Target cell 4C. Minimal biometric locks."

Carrick was already moving.

The door required a bypass. The lock had been upgraded from the floor plan Reyes had sourced, which was consistent with a facility that had been quietly expanded from its original footprint. Carrick handled it with the focused patience of someone who had bypassed worse. Thirty-eight seconds.

The room was eight feet by ten. Steel bed bolted to the floor. A sink with no mirror. A ceiling light that buzzed at a frequency calibrated to prevent deep sleep. Avril had seen rooms like this twice before, at different facilities, and the specific combination of details, the mirror's absence, the light's frequency, the bolted furniture, told him more about the facility's operating doctrine than anything in the procurement records.

The woman inside sat upright on the edge of the bed, hands in her lap, back straight. When the light from the hallway came in, she blinked once, slowly, the blink of someone who had learned to manage reactions, and then looked at Avril directly.

"You're not Marshals," she said.

"No," Avril said. "We're the follow-through."

She stood. Mid-thirties. Gaunt but clear-eyed. Her hair had been cut short at some point, unevenly. The stillness in her expression was the kind that came from burning through all the easier responses and arriving at something that ran on principle because principle was what was left.

"I'm Claire," she said. "Or that's what you're calling me today."

"Either way," Carrick said, already checking the corridor.

Avril held out the second uniform. She took it and changed quickly, unselfconsciously, the way people moved when modesty had become a resource they had stopped spending. Beneath her collar, old bruising, healed, not recent. He noted it and moved on.

"You brought the beacon?" she asked.

"You still have the payload?"

She reached into her mouth and produced a dental crown, rubber-capped. Inside: a flash drive thinner than a SIM card. She placed it in his hand like she was handing over something she had been keeping alive by holding it.

"Full schema," she said. "Codebase. Authorization chains. Not just the surveillance, but how they built it to stay outside court jurisdiction." She kept her voice flat and precise, the register of someone who had rehearsed this in a room with no one to say it to. "The system constructs false digital bridges. Makes targeted individuals appear to be foreign contacts. That designation activates SIGINT authority that would not otherwise apply. It's legally sanitized full-spectrum targeting. Citizens, made foreign by paperwork."

Avril put the drive in his jacket. He was thinking about the targeting criteria document, association with immigration advocacy organizations, and the specific legal mechanism Claire had just described. The mechanism that converted a civics teacher, or an immigration attorney, or a data analyst who flagged an audit, into a foreign contact. Not by what they did. By what the paperwork said they were.

He did not say this. He had learned, over months, that the moments when you understood the full shape of something were not the moments to speak. They were the moments to move.

"Last chance to say no," he said.

"I said yes when they locked me in," she said. "I just want air."

They moved.

They reached the secondary corridor without incident. The maintenance exit was thirty meters ahead, a dated mechanical lock, a false wall of supply carts and cleaning equipment. No camera coverage. The floor plan had shown this as the gap, and the floor plan had been right about everything else.

The guard appeared from a side corridor. Mid-twenties, the unfocused attention of someone working a shift he considered routine. His gaze passed over Avril, over Carrick, over Claire, and stopped on Eliana, who had moved inside to hold the exit while Reyes monitored the outer perimeter.

Not certainty. A question. His hand drifted toward the radio.

Eliana kept walking. She had the particular quality of someone who had spent years in courtrooms, oversight hearings, public proceedings, someone whose face had been visible in rooms where it cost something to be visible. She understood, in the fraction of a second, that the guard was processing what he thought he recognized, that stopping was the wrong response. You walked through recognition the way you walked through a checkpoint, without giving it what it needed to become a decision.

"Do I know you?" he said.

Carrick stepped into the line of sight between the guard and Claire. His voice was level. "Fiber drops down. We're running behind."

"I think I've seen you somewhere," the guard said, still looking at Eliana. "Some kind of"

"State oversight hearing," Eliana said, without breaking stride. "Probably. I've been to a lot of them." She said it the way you said something true to someone who was searching for something else, not a denial, not an invitation. Just a fact, offered and closed.

The guard's hand moved away from the radio.

"Right," he said. "Sure."

He turned back toward the corridor he had come from. Carrick waited three seconds, exactly three, and then they were moving again, through the exit, into the tunnel.

The tunnel was dark and narrow and smelled of old water and mineral rust. Avril flipped on his light. Claire walked without being told how. They moved fast without running, which was the difference between operational and panicked, and Avril had learned to hold that difference by feel rather than by thought.

"Daniels," he said quietly into the collar. "Any movement on the surveillance thread?"

A pause, two seconds, which was not Daniels' usual response time. "The ghost print fired. I have a timestamp."

"Match?"

"No," Daniels said. "That's what I need to tell you. It doesn't match the short list. The signature traces to a channel that's outside the team. Something that's been in the infrastructure longer than the network has existed."

Avril kept moving. He filed this the way he filed things that needed thinking rather than reaction, in the part of him that stayed open while the rest of him was doing something else.

"We talk when we're out," he said.

"Yes," Daniels said.

They reached the service hatch. Cold air. Trees. The van, half-buried in brush, exactly where Soto had left it.

They drove for an hour before anyone said anything that was not operational. Claire sat in the back with Avril, looking at the window with the focused attention of someone cataloguing things she had not seen in a long time: trees, a gas station, a billboard for a hardware store. The ordinary things. He did not interrupt that.

At the dead drop point, a shuttered produce stand on a stretch of rural road, a second vehicle waited with civilian clothes and documentation. Claire changed and stepped out. Before she left, she looked at Avril with the particular expression of someone who had made a calculation and arrived at something that was not quite gratitude, something more functional than that.

"Use it as it matters," she said, meaning the drive.

"Yes," he said.

She was gone in two minutes. The van continued east.

Back at the safehouse, Naomi was at the kitchen table. She had the atlas open, her daughter's atlas, the one she had been working through. Naomi was not reading it. She was looking at the page for Central America, which was where her daughter had stopped, and she was doing the thing Avril had noticed her doing every few days: staying very still in a specific way that was not peace but was the practice of it.

He sat across from her. She looked up.

"Clean?" she said.

"Clean," he said.

She nodded. They sat there for a moment in the particular quiet of two people who had each been inside different versions of the same long wait, and then Eliana came in from the exterior and started making coffee, and the moment passed into the room's general business.

Daniels brought it to him privately, which Avril had asked for and which Daniels had understood to mean: not in the room, not with the team listening, not as a briefing.

"The short list was wrong," Daniels said. He said it without preamble because the preamble was implicit in the choice to say it privately. "The signature traces to a relay that was in the network's infrastructure before the network launched. Not planted during an op. Not inserted through a channel we built. It was already there. Someone who had access to the underlying architecture, before the first safehouse, before the first contact, embedded a passive monitoring function. It's not reading. It's not collecting. It's flagging. Sending a pulse when specific operational sequences fire."

"To what address?" Avril said.

"I don't have the address yet. The pulse itself is routed through three layers. I can follow it, but it will take time, and I need to do it in a way that does not alert whoever is receiving."

Avril thought about the passive listener in SABLE_VERITY's relay. Placed before her defection by someone who knew the channel. He thought about the rotation schedule anomaly, the channel's history, and the provenance that predated her decision to leave. He thought about the thing he and Carrick had named and left sitting two weeks ago because it needed to sit before they could look at it directly.

"The problem," he said slowly, "is not inside the team. It is underneath the team. Someone built access into the infrastructure before we built the team."

"Yes," Daniels said.

"Which means they knew what the network was going to be before it existed."

"Or they seeded enough infrastructure to be in position when something like it was built," Daniels said. "Either way, the access predates us."

They sat with that for a moment.

"Keep following it," Avril said. "Carefully. Don't pull on it until you know where it ends."

"Yes," Daniels said. He left without further comment, which was correct.

Avril stayed at the table. He put the flash drive on the surface in front of him and looked at it. Then he picked it up, put it in an opaque lead sleeve, and took it to a transit hub forty minutes away, a public facility, busy enough that one person leaving a locker was invisible. He placed the drive in locker 23B. The retrieval code had been sent to Trina Cole through SABLE_VERITY's verified channel an hour before the op, with a single line: When you have it, you'll have everything.

He put Common Sense in the locker alongside the drive, not as a symbol, as cover, something for the locker to look like it contained. He closed the door.

On the way back, he thought about Lina Alvarez. Twenty-seven. Civics teacher. The van doors. He thought about the mechanism Claire had described, citizens made foreign by paperwork, and whether it had a name somewhere in a document that described her exactly. He thought about how long the machine had been running before any of them knew to look back, and how the relay in the infrastructure had been there before the network, which meant the machine had been watching for the network before the network knew it was a network.

He thought about Trina Cole in whatever room she was in, waiting for something she had agreed to verify without knowing how much of it there was.

She was about to find out. He drove back through the dark without the radio on, thinking about what it meant that the infrastructure had been seeded from before the beginning, and what it would mean to follow that thread to the end.

Chapter Twenty: The Leak

The documentation had gone public at 2:17 in the morning, which she knew because she had been awake and watching the indicators when the first mirror site went live. She had spent the three hours since then watching the cascade, the amplification, the deepfakes, the hostile channels picking up fragments and repackaging them, the verified material buried under a thousand distorted copies, with the particular stillness of someone who had expected something like this and still found it worse than expected.

What she had not expected was the timing of the second thing.

Trina Cole had been detained at 5:04 in the morning. Not charged. Detained. The distinction was the kind the administration had been erasing for two years, which meant it was the kind that still mattered to her.

She looked at the name in her coat pocket. The paper she had not burned. She had been carrying the distinction, witness, not traitor, for three days without acting on it, and now the distinction had a deadline attached.

If Trina Cole disappeared into the system the way the others had disappeared, the verified case disappeared with her. The chain of evidence Trina had been building, the treaty compliance files, the targeting criteria document, Claire's flash drive, the Layer Nine procurement chain, existed in Trina's work and in SABLE_VERITY's documentation, and nowhere else that a courtroom would accept. The leak had put the raw data into the world. Without the chain of evidence, the raw data were just noise. The kind of noise the machine knew how to produce more of.

She picked up the phone.

This time, she routed it.

The message from SABLE_VERITY arrived at the terminal at 5:40 in the morning, six words after the authentication header: TRINA COLE DETAINED. SAME RELAY. SAME HAND.

Avril read it standing up, still in what he had slept in, which was almost everything he had been wearing the night before. Mason was already at the monitoring station. He had been up for two hours, watching the documentation spread across platforms and jurisdictions with the focused attention of someone cataloguing a disaster rather than reacting to one.

"SABLE_VERITY's saying the relay that triggered the release is the one she found the passive listener in," Avril said.

"I know," Mason said, without looking up. "I pulled the relay log twenty minutes ago. Daniels has been tracing it since 0300. He has something."

Avril went to find Daniel.

He was at the secondary terminal in the back room, the one with the hardened uplink, in the same posture he occupied when he was working through something he had not finished yet, elbows on the table, the particular stillness of someone whose mind was running faster than everything else.

"Remote trigger," he said when Avril came in. "Not automatic. Not a dead-man switch. Someone with access to the pre-existing infrastructure saw the data moving through the relay and made a decision. They waited until the documentation was assembled, all of it, the treaty compliance files, the targeting criteria, the flash drive contents, and then they released it."

"Who?" Avril said.

"I cannot name them yet. But the trigger point narrows the window. The person who released it had access to the relay's control layer. That access was built in when the relay was seeded, before the network launched. The same person who built the passive listener into SABLE_VERITY's channel, the same person who put the ghost print in the CSI-7 transfer sequence." He paused. "Same hand throughout. They have been inside the infrastructure since before we used it. And they chose now to act."

"Why now?" Avril said.

"Because the case was complete," Daniels said. He said it without inflection, the way he said things that were bad but accurate. "They waited until all the pieces were assembled in one place, the full documentation chain, and then they released it. Not the verified version. Not Trina's controlled publication. Just the raw data, through channels designed to maximize dispersion and minimize attribution."

"They wanted it out," Avril said. "But not in a form anyone could use."

"They wanted the information to be public, but the case was destroyed," Daniels said. "Those are different objectives. The first makes the truth available. The second makes it unprovable."

Avril stood with that for a moment.

"Keep following the access trail," he said. "And tell me when you can name them."

"Yes," Daniels said. He was already looking back at the screen.

Then, after a moment, he said something else, not looking up, his voice carrying the flat register he used when a fact was bad but had not yet resolved into its full implications.

"There is something else in the access logs. Separate from the relay trigger. A monitoring flag activation, passive watch designation, not a collection event. Something in the We Resist orbit that had been dormant was reclassified six weeks ago. The flag tripped and the record updated." A pause. "I do not know what caused it yet. The trigger event is not in the access log, just the activation."

Avril said nothing.

"Six weeks ago," Daniels said again. He said it the second time, the way he said things that had more than one possible explanation, and was waiting for Avril to tell him which one was operative. "Do you know what happened six weeks ago that might have touched a passive watch designation?"

Avril looked at the table. He knew the timestamp. He had not needed Daniels to tell him. The number had arrived in his chest before Daniels finished the sentence, landing in the specific place where things you already knew but had not named yet lived until someone named them for you.

"Keep following it," he said. "Everything you can reach."

"Yes," Daniels said.

Avril left the room. He stood in the corridor for a moment with his hand on the wall.

By seven in the morning, Mason had the feeds up in parallel, a dozen sources in as many languages, each one running its own version of the same documentation.

The Spanish outlet was straightforward: raw data, minimal editorialising, the kind of coverage that assumed its readers were capable of reading a procurement chain. The Russian state channel had already reframed it as evidence of American internal collapse, which was not wrong about what it showed but was wrong about what it meant. Three domestic networks were running the foreign operatives line with enough repetition to make it feel like an established fact. A think tank had produced, in less than six hours, a detailed analysis of why the documentation was fabricated, citing no specific errors, but citing the pattern of fabricated documents in general.

And then there was the composite.

Mason pulled it up without comment. A video, timestamped two hours after the leak: Avril's face, Avril's voice, an outdoor setting he did not recognize, saying, "We will dismantle their republic by any means necessary. Burn the network. Burn it all."

The audio was his voice. The words were not.

Eliana, who had come in while Mason was pulling up the feeds, watched the composite play. When it finished, she said, "They built this before the leak. You do not turn around a deepfake this clean in two hours."

"No," Mason agreed. "Someone had the composite ready. The leak was the trigger."

"So whoever released the data also prepared the counter-narrative," Avril said.

"Or whoever released the data knew the counter-narrative was already prepared and chose this moment because of it," Eliana said. "Same outcome. A different question about how many people knew."

Avril watched the composite on loop for one more pass, his face saying things he had never said, his voice saying them in his exact cadence, and then turned away from it.

"What about Trina?" he said.

"SABLE_VERITY says detained. No charge filed. The channel has been cold since 0500." Mason's voice was level, which was how he delivered things he could not fix. "She completed the verification before the relay fired. The connection exists; she made it. But without her to present it and attest to the chain of evidence, its provenance can be attacked. The verified case is intact. It is just inaccessible."

Eliana looked at Avril. "If she disappears the way the others have disappeared."

"She will not," Avril said. He said it before he had a reason to believe it. Then, more carefully, "Someone is deciding that right now."

Carrick had been listening from the doorway, which was where he processed things he was still deciding about. When he came into the room fully, the team arranged itself around him the way it always did, not by direction, just by the gravity of what he was about to say.

"Someone chose to release this," he said. "Not the team. Not Trina. Not an accident. Someone who has been inside the infrastructure since before the network existed made a deliberate decision last night to put the documentation into the world in a form that would maximize damage and minimize verifiability." He looked at Avril. "That person has had access to our operations since the beginning. They watched us assemble the case. They knew what we were building. And they decided that the right moment to release it was when the verified version was complete, and the counter-narrative was already in place."

The room was quiet for a long moment.

"You are saying they used us," Reyes said.

"I am saying someone did," Carrick said. "I am not saying who. I am saying that is the shape of it."

"The shape of it," Eliana said slowly, "is that the truth is out, Trina is detained, the verified case is inaccessible, and someone with access to our infrastructure made all three things happen simultaneously." She looked at the feed still running on Mason's screen. "What they released was real. The data is real. They didn't fabricate it. They just released it in the worst possible way."

"Why release real data badly?" Reyes said.

"Because real data badly released is harder to fix than fabricated data," Daniels said from the doorway. He had come in at some point without anyone marking the moment. "A fabrication can be proven false. A real dataset released without provenance or context, in a form designed to be amplified by hostile actors and buried under deepfakes, that's much harder to rehabilitate."

"You can discredit the truth without lying about it," Eliana said. "Just release it wrong."

Nobody spoke after that for a while. The feeds ran. The composite played somewhere in the background. Outside, the morning was ordinary.

Naomi was at the kitchen table when Avril came through. She had the atlas open again, not her daughter's page this time, but an earlier one. Europe. She was looking at something on the page with the focused attention she brought to things she was trying to understand rather than things she already knew.

The composite was playing on the small screen in the corner, the sound off. Avril's face, his voice, saying things he had never said. Naomi glanced at it once, then looked back at the atlas.

"Carlos," Avril said. "Reyes is still working on it."

She nodded. She did not say that she knew, or that she was patient, or that she understood. She just nodded, which was the whole of it.

He sat down across from her. The atlas was open to a spread of coastlines, the same kind of spread, he realized, that Lena's scarf had been folded on top of months ago, in the early days, when he had still been learning what kind of thing he was building.

He sat there for a while without saying anything, the feeds audible from the other room, Mason's voice listing sources and timestamps with the flat precision of someone accounting for what could be accounted for. The composite played on the small screen in the corner. His face. His voice. Someone else's words.

He thought about Lina Alvarez. Twenty-seven. Civics teacher. Her name was called out as the van doors closed. He had started building the network with a single video and a single name, because the thing that had happened to her had been documented, and the documentation had existed, and he had understood that documentation was the difference between a thing that happened and a thing that could be proven to have happened.

What the person who seeded the infrastructure had understood, and what they had been patient enough to wait for, was that documentation could be released in a way that made it harder to believe that the difference between a thing being provable and a thing being proven was the chain of custody, the verified source, the journalist who could attest to the connection and present it to an audience that trusted her. They had taken Trina Cole. They had released the data without her. The documentation existed, was real, was accurate, and was now surrounded by so much noise that the path from raw data to proven fact had been made deliberately impassable.

The machine's ability to make things disappear had always been matched by its ability to make things appear. He had understood the first. He had underestimated the second.

He took the scarf out of his jacket pocket. Cedar and ink, nearly nothing. He held it.

He thought about the decision he had made three weeks ago, not the network, not the extractions, but the specific operational choice to wait until the documentation was complete before moving it. Hold until everything is verified. Hold until Trina had the treaty compliance files and the targeting criteria and Claire's flash drive and the Layer Nine chain, hold until the case was whole, not partial.

He had made that call because partial cases got discredited, because the thing he was building needed to be unassailable, because he had learned from the Lina Alvarez footage and from Trina's warning and from every file he had ever built that a half-case was worse than no case. He had been right about that. He was still right about that.

And the person who had seeded the infrastructure had been watching him be right about it. Had waited, specifically, for the moment when the case was complete. Had used his carefulness as the trigger condition. The decision that had made the documentation most valuable had also made it most exploitable, because a partial case, released early, would have been less damaging to release badly.

It was the completeness that made the timing devastating.

He had done the right thing. The right thing had cost them Trina, the chain of custody, and the verified path from raw data to proven fact. Both of those were true at the same time. A third thing was also true, and he was not yet ready to look at it directly: that three weeks earlier, he had done something that had nothing to do with carefulness, and that it had cost someone he loved, and that the two mistakes together, the careful one and the reflexive one, had been running in parallel the whole time, serving the same machine. He did not know how to hold them both yet. He understood he was going to have to.

From the other room, Daniels had a second relay node. He was narrowing it.

Avril put the scarf back. He stood.

The documentation was out. The case was intact but buried. Trina was detained. The path from here to the thing being proven was longer than it had been yesterday, and the person who had made it longer had been inside the infrastructure since before the network knew it was a network.

He went back to the table where Daniels was working.

Chapter Twenty-One: The Mole

Forty-eight hours had passed since she had routed the call. In that time, she had done three things: she had placed Trina Cole in a different category, not detained, not free, held in the particular liminal space that her institution used when it wanted to protect something without admitting it was protecting it. She had started a trace on the relay. And she had not slept.

The relay trace was the one that was keeping her up.

The architecture was familiar in the way that things from your own past were familiar, not comfortable, not welcome, but immediately recognisable. The relay's structure bore the fingerprints of a program she had worked adjacent to in her third year at the agency, a program whose classification she had never been given but whose outputs she had reviewed. It had been running under a designation she had not seen in fifteen years.

She pulled the classification record. It required three separate authentications, and one she did not technically have clearance for, which she handled the way she handled most things that required something she was not supposed to have: carefully, indirectly, through a request that would not be logged in a way that connected back to her name.

The record came back. She read the designation. She read it again.

It was older than Tower Sentinel. It was older than the program that had produced Tower Sentinel. It was the origin of everything she had spent three years trying to trace.

She sat alone in her office with this for a long time. Then she made a note, on paper, in a drawer, and went back to work.

The signal came through at 0320, on a frequency Mason had flagged three days earlier as a ghost layer, old spectrum, unused since the early days of the network, the kind of band that only existed in their configuration because Avril had set it up before he understood what he was building and never taken it down.

Mason caught it. He brought it to Avril without comment, which was how he brought things that had weight.

The transmission was forty-one seconds. The first twelve were static degradation, the signature of a signal that had been relayed through four or five nodes before reaching them. Then a voice, compressed and slightly distorted but recognisable to Avril from the municipal archive in Geneva and the dead-drop relay in the months since.

"RAVEN contact. Channels burned. Using a ghost layer, one transmission, no repeat. My network has the relay. Not the address, the origin program. Classification NOMAD. Pre-Tower Sentinel. Pre-everything you know. Whoever runs NOMAD has been running it since before the network launched. Maybe before you decided to build the network, you should have looked at who knew what you were going to build before you knew."

A burst of static. Then silence.

Avril played it twice. The second time, he stood very still and listened to the part he had almost missed the first time: before you decided to build the network. Not before the network launched. Before he decided.

"Grey Sentinel," Mason said.

"Yes."

"He's been dark since the seminary."

"Yes."

Mason looked at the console. "His regular channels would have been burned when the data leaked; the relay's architecture would have compromised anything that touched it. He would have known that. He waited until he had something specific enough to justify a ghost transmission."

"Which means what he found is specific," Avril said. "Get Daniels."

Daniels had been following the access trail for six days. He came in, sat down, and set a printout on the table without preamble, a single page with three-column entries, the kind of document generated by a system rather than written by a person.

"NOMAD," he said. "That's what the relay calls itself. Not a person, a program. A persistent monitoring and intervention function, seeded into the infrastructure before the network launched. It ran passively until the complete documentation was assembled in one place. Then it triggered: remote release, deliberate degradation of the verification chain. Both functions are native to the program's architecture; it was built to do both."

"Built by whom?" Avril said.

"I have the classification now," Daniels said. "Grey Sentinel's transmission confirms it. NOMAD is a pre-Tower Sentinel program. It predates the surveillance architecture We Resist has been documenting. It's the mechanism by which the apparatus learns to anticipate resistance movements before they organize. Not by monitoring them, but by positioning itself inside the infrastructure they will eventually use."

"It waited for us to build the network," Avril said. "Then it moved in."

"It may have been waiting for something like the network for years," Daniels said. "The relay architecture that NOMAD uses appears in infrastructure records from seventeen years ago. Whoever built it was patient."

Avril looked at the printout. NOMAD. A program older than the surveillance architecture they had spent months documenting, older than Tower Sentinel, built specifically to do what had been done to them.

"Who controls it now?" he said.

"I do not know yet," Daniels said. "The program classification traces to an administrative entity that no longer exists under that name. I need more time to follow the chain."

"How much time."

"Days. Maybe a week."

"You have days," Avril said. "Not a week."

He brought it to the team the way he brought things that required a decision: fully, without softening it. Grey Sentinel's transmission. Daniels' NOMAD classification. The convergence of the two. The fact that the program had been seeded into their infrastructure before the network existed and had been monitoring them had, in a sense, been waiting for them, since before they knew there was anything to wait for.

Carrick listened to all of it. When Avril finished, he was quiet for a long moment.

"Grey Sentinel has been dark for three months," he said. "His regular channels burned in the leak. He reappears on a ghost layer with intelligence that directly addresses the threat we have been working on for six days." He paused. "The timing is either very good or very constructed."

"The transmission had physical degradation," Mason said. "Four or five relay hops. That is not something you manufacture cleanly."

"You can manufacture degradation," Carrick said. "You cannot manufacture everything."

Eliana had been listening from the doorway. She came in now, slowly, the way she came in when she was carrying something she had been working through.

"NOMAD was built to position itself inside the infrastructure of resistance movements before they organize," she said. "Which means it has been inside networks like this one before. Which means there are other networks that were compromised in the same way. Some of them may still exist."

The room took that in.

"If NOMAD is the architecture," she continued, "then what it did to us, leaked the data, degraded the case, detained Trina, those are not the end of the operation. Those are the middle. The end is whatever comes after."

"And we do not know what comes after," Reyes said.

"No," Eliana said, "which is why we need Grey Sentinel to finish the transmission."

"He said one transmission, no repeat," Mason said.

"He said that using a ghost layer," Avril said. "He is still out there. He has not gone to ground; he found something specific enough to transmit and then went quiet to see who responded. If we signal back through the ghost layer, he will know we heard it."

"And if someone else is watching the ghost layer," Carrick said, "they will know we did."

The room held this. Naomi was at the table in the corner. She had been there since the briefing started, the atlas closed in front of her, her hands folded on top of it. She did not speak. But the fact of her sitting there, waiting for something that was taking longer than anyone had told her it would take, was present in the room the way facts like that were present.

"We signal back," Avril said. "Ghost layer, no content, just an acknowledgement. He will know we heard him. If he has more, he will find a way to get it to us."

Carrick looked at him for a moment. Then he turned to Mason. "Do it."

The acknowledgement went out at 0610. Mason watched the ghost layer for two hours and then reported nothing, no response, no indication the frequency was being monitored by anyone other than themselves, which was either clean or the kind of clean that was itself a signal.

Daniels had spent the time since the briefing following the NOMAD classification chain. He came back at midday with one more entry from the administrative records, a cross-reference that connected the program classification to a budget line that had been active from the program's inception through a reorganisation that had occurred, his timeline showed, eight months before Avril had posted the first document to the We Resist server.

"The budget line," Daniels said, "ran through a sub-entity of an entity that no longer exists. The sub-entity was dissolved in the same reorganisation. But the dissolution records list it as absorbed, not closed. Absorbed into a current operating unit."

"Which unit?" Avril said.

Daniels looked at him. "I do not have the unit name yet. The absorption record is classified above my current access level. I would need a week and a significant institutional credential to get to it cleanly."

"Or someone on the inside with the right clearance," Mason said quietly. He was not looking at Avril when he said it. He was looking at the monitor where Grey Sentinel's transmission had come in.

The room understood what he meant. They did not say it directly.

Avril thought about the NSA Advisor. About the name in her coat pocket. About the call she had routed two days ago through institutional channels, and what routing a call through institutional channels with that name meant for someone who had spent a career learning when to move through the institution and when to hold outside it.

He thought about two investigations approaching the same point from opposite ends, with no knowledge of each other and no way to communicate directly.

"Keep following the chain," he told Daniels. "Everything you can reach without triggering an alert. We note where you stop, and we figure out how to cover the gap."

"Yes," Daniels said.

That evening, Avril sat with the day's accumulated facts. NOMAD. A program older than Tower Sentinel, built to seed itself into resistance infrastructure before it launched. Grey Sentinel's transmission. The convergence of his network's intelligence with Daniels' access trace. The budget line was absorbed into a current operating unit with a classification above Daniels' reach. The NSA Advisor, somewhere in the institution, is following the same thread from the other direction.

And Trina Cole, held in the liminal space between detained and free, her verified case intact in a form that required her presence to be usable.

He thought about Lina Alvarez. Twenty-seven. Civics teacher. Her name was called out as the van doors closed twenty-three seconds into a video that had made him build the thing that NOMAD had been waiting to seed itself into. He thought about the patience of it, the relay in the infrastructure, seventeen years of architecture, the program built to wait for resistance to organize so it could be inside the resistance before it knew it was a resistance.

The machine had not been watching Lina Alvarez because she was dangerous. It had been watching the infrastructure she was adjacent to, the networks she was part of, the organising she was connected to, because those were the seeds of something the machine had learned to intercept before they grew. She had disappeared not because of what she knew but because of what the network around her was about to become.

He had not known that when he started. He understood it now.

He opened the notebook to a fresh page. He wrote the classification: NOMAD. He wrote the date range from Daniels' record, seventeen years. He wrote: absorbed, not closed. He wrote: current operating unit.

He did not write what he was beginning to understand about who had built it. He was not yet ready to write that down. But he left space.

From the other room, Naomi's daughter had asked Eliana something about the atlas, one of the countries on the Central America page, a capital city and a question about whether people there spoke the same language as in Honduras. Eliana's voice, low and patient, was explaining.

Avril listened to this for a moment. Then he closed the notebook and went to sit with them.

Chapter Twenty-Two: Containment

Three days, two accesses she shouldn't have, and one that required her to use a credential that existed only because she had never officially relinquished it when the program it belonged to was dissolved. The credential still worked. She had not been certain it would.

The unit name was on her screen for thirty seconds before she wrote it down on paper and cleared the record. Thirty seconds was longer than she needed. She had spent the additional time looking at it.

The entity that controlled NOMAD was not a surveillance program. It was not a counterintelligence function. It was not any of the categories she had been using to think about it. It was something older than those categories, a foundational operating unit whose stated purpose, in the original classification documents she was reading for the first time, was described in language she recognized from the earliest years of the apparatus: continuity of governance through anticipatory stabilisation.

Not watching resistance. Preventing the conditions under which resistance became possible.

She had thought she was tracing a surveillance architecture. She had found something that predated the surveillance architecture by twenty years. NOMAD was not the machine watching them.

NOMAD was the machine that had built the conditions that made watching them seem necessary.

She sat with this for a while. Then she wrote the unit name on a second piece of paper. She addressed it through a channel she had not used in eleven years. She sent it.

She did not know if anyone on the other end would receive it. She did not know if the channel was still active. She knew only that she had, over the past three weeks, done four things the institution did not know she had done, and that the fifth thing, which would be to bring the unit name into the institution, was the one that would make all the others visible. She was not ready for that.

Not yet.

It came through at 0840, not on the ghost layer they had acknowledged but on a different channel, one that Avril had built in the network's first year, before he had understood what he was building, that had been dormant since the third month of operations. A channel that existed only in the original network architecture files, which were on hardware he had not touched in over a year.

Mason flagged it immediately, which was the correct procedure, and then held it for four minutes while he ran a provenance check, which was also the correct procedure. When he brought it to Avril, he said, "The channel provenance is clean. Pre-network architecture, inactive since month three. Someone who had access to the original configuration files used it."

"Who has those files?" Avril said.

"We do. Grey Sentinel doesn't. Or shouldn't." Mason's expression was careful. "Unless someone gave them to him. Or someone with access to the original files is operating under his designation."

Avril read the message.

"RAVEN. UNIT NAME REQUIRES IN-PERSON TRANSFER. CHANNEL RISK BEYOND THIS POINT UNACCEPTABLE. LOCATION FOLLOWS. ONE-TIME WINDOW: 72 HOURS. COME ALONE OR WITH ONE PERSON YOU TRUST ENTIRELY. I WILL NOT BE COMING BACK AFTER THIS."

A set of coordinates followed. A city three hours away. A building designation. A time.

"He's not coming back," Mason said.

"No."

"The channel provenance means someone with access to our original architecture is involved. That's either a problem or an explanation."

Avril looked at the coordinates. "Get Carrick," he said.

Daniels came in mid-morning with the flat expression he used when he had a fact that was not the fact he had been trying to find.

"The absorption record is one classification level above my current access," he said. "I can reach it laterally. There are adjacent records that imply the unit name, but I can't pull the record itself without triggering an alert. If I trigger an alert, whoever monitors the NOMAD architecture will know someone is looking for them."

"And they'll know from where," Avril said.

"Yes."

"So we stop."

"For now," Daniels said. "Unless something changes the access picture."

Something changed the access picture at 1140.

SABLE_VERITY's message came through her verified channel at the Sanctuary node, not from the network, but to it. Mason read it twice before he called Avril.

The message was from a former colleague she had identified only by a program designation she and Avril had not seen before: HARBOR. The text was three sentences: **THE UNIT NAME IS DIRECTORATE ELEVEN. I FOUND IT FROM MY SIDE. I EXPECT YOU FOUND IT FROM YOURS. I THINK WE ARE OUT OF TIME."**

SABLE_VERITY had added one line of her own: "I know this person. They were in the room on July 7th."

Avril read this standing at the terminal. He stood there for a long time.

July 7th. The night someone inside the apparatus had triggered the abort flare. The night SABLE_VERITY had been in the room. The night the journalists from Tower Sentinel's target list had been given one night to move.

The person who had triggered the flare, who had bought them one night, at a cost that had followed them into a sealed program and then into whatever HARBOR designated, had just reached across eleven years to give them a name.

"Daniels," Avril said.

Daniels looked at the message and was quiet for a long moment. Then he said, "Directorate Eleven. That designation appears in the Tower Sentinel documentation. Not as an operator. As the originating authority."

The room took that in without speaking.

"It's not the surveillance architecture," Daniels said. "It's what authorized the surveillance architecture. It's what authorized Tower Sentinel. It's what NOMAD was built to serve."

"How long has it existed?" Eliana said from the doorway.

"Based on the Tower Sentinel documentation," Daniels said, "at least thirty years."

Carrick listened to all of it, the channel provenance, Grey Sentinel's message, Directorate Eleven, HARBOR, with the particular stillness of someone cataloguing threat before they assessed it.

"The channel Grey Sentinel used requires access to our original architecture files," he said, when Avril finished. "Which means either someone inside our network gave them to him, or someone operating under his designation had them already. The first option means we have an exposure we haven't identified. The second option means Grey Sentinel is not the only person using that handle."

"Or both," Reyes said.

"Or both," Carrick agreed. "Going to a one-time physical meeting with a contact whose channel provenance we can't fully explain, while we're simultaneously holding the name of the entity that built the machine we've been fighting, that's the kind of moment the machine was built to exploit."

"And if we don't go," Eliana said, "we lose whatever he's carrying that's too dangerous to transmit. He said he's not coming back. That's not tradecraft language, that's someone who is out of time."

"HARBOR is out of time, too," Mason said. "They reached across eleven years through SABLE_VERITY's channel. They were in the room on July 7th. If Directorate Eleven is still active and HARBOR knows the unit name, HARBOR is at risk the same way SABLE_VERITY was."

Reyes said, "We go, we go with full counter-surveillance. We treat it as hostile until proven otherwise. We don't bring anything that connects back to the safehouse."

Carrick looked at Avril. "One person you trust entirely. That's what he said."

"Yes," Avril said.

A silence. They all understood what the silence meant.

"Seventy-two hours," Carrick said. "We have time to prepare."

"Forty-eight," Avril said. "We leave a buffer. If the meeting is compromised, we need room to move."

Carrick nodded once. That was the decision.

He found Naomi in the kitchen that evening. The atlas was on the table, open. Not to the Central America page. Her daughter had moved past it. This page was Honduras. The capital city. The roads run inland toward the Nicaraguan border. Her daughter had drawn a small star in pencil at a point in the mountains, and written a word beside it in careful child's handwriting that Avril had to lean in to read.

It said, "papi."

Naomi saw him looking. She didn't explain it. She closed the atlas with the page marked, a strip of paper she'd torn from the corner of a receipt, and set it aside.

"Reyes says he has a lead," Avril said. "Not a window yet. A lead."

She nodded. The nod was the same one she had given him in the van, in the corridor, in every moment since Louisville, where the answer had been not yet. He had stopped trying to supplement it with words.

He sat down across from her. On the table between them: the atlas, closed. A cup of coffee that had gone cold. The receipt strip she'd used as a bookmark.

He thought about what it meant that Directorate Eleven had a thirty-year history and that NOMAD had been built to serve it and that the relay had been seeded into the infrastructure eight months before the first We Resist document and that the machine had known what the network would become before the network did. He thought about Lina Alvarez, twenty-seven, civics teacher, and the network around her that had been flagged by an entity that had been doing this for thirty years, to networks before hers, and would do it to networks after. The machine did not need to identify individuals. It needed to prevent the conditions under which the individuals became a network. Lina Alvarez had been adjacent to the seed of something. That was enough.

He took the paper with Directorate Eleven's name on it out of his jacket pocket. He folded it once and set it on the table next to the scarf, which had no smell left at all now, just the shape of itself, the cedar and ink entirely gone.

He looked at both of them for a moment. Then he put them both back.

"Your daughter's map is good," he said.

Naomi looked at him. "She found it on the Honduras page. She said the star is where she thinks he is." A pause. "She didn't ask me if that was right."

"Is it?" he said.

She considered the question with the seriousness it deserved. "Close," she said.

He nodded. They sat there for a while in the particular quiet of two people who had run out of the easier things to say and had arrived, through exhaustion and proximity, at something that didn't require words to be present.

In the other room, Mason's voice, flat, functional, the register of someone running a check. Daniels typing. The sounds of the work continuing, which was what it did.

He stayed at the table after Naomi went to bed. The kitchen had its quiet: the monitor running in the other room, the occasional sound of Mason adjusting something, the building settling into its late-night register.

He took out the SHADOW document, not to add to it, just to look. Eleven entries over seven months. Three deleted: Mason's two, and one early entry about a routing anomaly that had resolved into a hardware fault. What remained was a record of suspicion shaped by evidence into something narrower and more specific: not who, not yet, but the outline of how. The relay. The timing. The patience of it.

There was a twelfth entry he hadn't written. He knew what it would say. He knew the timestamp, the mechanism, the outcome. He had not written it because doing so would make it a fact in the record, and he was not ready for it to be one. He closed the document without writing anything. He understood that not writing it was also a decision, and that the decision said something about him he didn't want to read.

He opened the monitoring thread logs. Not looking for anything specific, the way you reviewed logs at the end of a long day, checking for anomalies before closing out. The logs from the night the documentation went live. He'd been through them twice in the first forty-eight hours. He hadn't been through them since.

The timestamp was at 2:31 in the morning, forty-three minutes before the first mirror site went live. A flag in Mason's monitoring thread: a pre-release signal, origin masked, indicating the documentation was about to move. A signal Mason had been watching for, because it was the kind of signal that preceded a significant infrastructure event.

The next entry in Mason's log was 2:49 in the morning, six minutes after the first mirror site went live.

Eighteen minutes. Eighteen minutes between the signal and the next log entry, during which Mason had received advance warning that the documentation release was imminent, had not woken Avril, had not sent a message to any channel, and had made a decision alone in the monitoring station while the safehouse slept.

Avril sat with it for a long time. He understood what decision Mason had made, and he understood why. If Avril had known with eighteen minutes to spare, he would have tried to stop the release, pull the documentation back, buy time and protect the verification chain. That would have been the wrong call. The release was already in motion; pulling it would have fragmented the chain without stopping the deepfakes, and the case would have been worse, not better. Mason had assessed this correctly. Mason had decided alone.

He sat with what Mason had done and tried to be honest about it. The call had been correct. He could see that clearly, could trace the logic: eighteen minutes was not enough to pull the documentation back cleanly, and a fragmented release would have been worse than the one that happened. Mason had understood this alone in the dark while the safehouse slept, and had made the right decision without waking anyone to share the weight of it. That was what made it hard to sit with. Not the decision, but the aloneness of it. Mason had looked at the situation, run the same calculus Avril would have run, reached the correct answer, and then carried it quietly for six days while Avril deleted his name from the SHADOW document and told himself the question was settled. The question had not been settled. It had simply moved somewhere Avril hadn't thought to look. He was not sure what to do with the knowledge that Mason had protected the mission by keeping a secret from the person who ran it, that the secret had been right to keep, and that both were true and neither canceled the other.

He closed the log. He didn't add anything to the SHADOW document. He didn't open it. He sat in the dark kitchen with the fact of it, the fact of the unwritten twelfth entry, and the fact that he was going into a room in forty-eight hours to receive a name, carrying things Mason didn't know he knew and that he was not going to say.

He took out the notebook. He read the last entry, Directorate Eleven. Thirty years. NOMAD was built to serve it, and then looked at the blank page below it for a while.

He had built We Resist because the documentation existed and needed a place to live. He had built it because Lina Alvarez had called out her own name as the van doors closed, and the record deserved to carry that name. He had not built it, expecting to find the machine beneath the machine, the thing that had built the conditions for everything he had been documenting, that had been doing this since before he understood what it was doing, that had placed a listening architecture inside his network before the network existed.

He had not built it, expecting the name. He was going to receive the name in forty-eight hours, in a room with a person who had pulled an abort flare on July 7th and had lived with that decision for eleven years. A person who had reached across all of that to give them the one thing the record still needed.

He thought about what the name would mean. Not the end of anything. He was not naive enough to believe that. A name in a record was what he had spent two years learning to build, and he understood by then the precise distance between a name in a record and a name that had been answered for. That distance was the length of the book he had been writing. He was not going to pretend the distance was shorter than it was.

But the name would be in the record. And the record would be there.

He took out the scarf. There was almost nothing left. The fabric had thinned to translucent at the folds, the shape held by habit rather than structure. He had been carrying it for two years. He had pressed it to a wound in Horizon Park and not thought of it as an act. He had carried it through every operation, every safehouse, every late night at every table. It had no smell. It had no warmth. What it had was the fact of having been hers, and of having been his long enough that the distinction had blurred.

He held it for a while. Then he folded it carefully, four folds, the way he had always folded it, and put it back.

He opened the notebook to a fresh page. He wrote one sentence.

He closed the notebook and left it on the table.

In forty-eight hours, he would be in a room with a person who had waited eleven years to give someone a name. He would be ready. He would go in knowing what the name would and wouldn't change, what it would and wouldn't answer for, what it would cost to have waited this long, and what it would cost to receive it.

He was not going to look away.

He turned off the kitchen light and went to the door of the other room, where Mason was still running checks. Still working. He stood there for a moment, watching him work.

Then he went to bed.

Chapter Twenty-Three: The Enemy Within

The response to her transmission came back in 18 hours, indicating the channel was still active. What it told her beyond that took longer to understand.

The response did not come from the person she had sent it to. She didn't know who she had sent it to. The channel had been dormant for eleven years. The address had belonged to a program that no longer existed under that name, and she had not known with any certainty that anyone was still monitoring it. Someone was. And the person who replied was not operating under any designation she had authorized.

The reply contained four words and a number: "AWAITING YOUR NEXT STEP. 7."

The number seven. In the operational notation of the program she had worked on fifteen years ago, seven was a location designation, a dead-drop address that had been active during a specific operational period. She had not used it. She knew it because she had reviewed its usage logs during an internal audit in her third year. The logs had shown one authorized user during the relevant period.

The person who had sent her this response had been inside Directorate Eleven.

She sat with this for a long time. The possibilities were: someone currently inside who had been watching for this kind of contact and was now offering access, someone formerly inside who had been waiting for a transmission on this channel for years, or a trap built by whoever was running Directorate Eleven's current operations, designed to identify precisely the kind of institutional actor who would go looking for the unit name through unauthorized channels.

All three possibilities required the same response: careful movement, nothing logged, and the particular patience of someone who had learned that rushing toward a source made sources liabilities.

She did not reply. She noted the location designation on paper. She put it in her coat with the other papers.

She had now done five things the institution didn't know she had done.

The building was a former insurance records archive in a mid-sized city, slowly emptying since the decade it was built. Six floors, climate-controlled when it was in operation, the kind of structure that attracted nothing now because there was nothing to attract. The address had been in Grey Sentinel's message. The floor and room number had followed in a separate transmission, twelve hours later, which was either tradecraft or the kind of caution that came from someone who had been doing this long enough to know that the gap between a meeting invitation and the meeting itself was when most things went wrong.

Carrick swept the building before Avril entered. Three circuits, forty minutes, the particular thoroughness of someone for whom this was not methodology but instinct. He came back with nothing, which was either reassuring or the best possible staging for a trap, and said so in exactly those words.

"I know," Avril said. "We go in anyway."

They went in anyway.

Grey Sentinel was on the fourth floor, in a room that still had a desk and two chairs and a window so grimy it admitted light without admitting anything else. He was standing when they arrived, not sitting, the posture of someone who had decided standing was less of a commitment. Beside him, in the second chair, was a woman.

She was in her early sixties. The stillness in her was the particular kind that came from spending years learning how to be in a room without the room knowing you were there. She looked at Avril when he came through the door with the attention of someone who had been thinking about this meeting for a long time.

"HARBOR," Grey Sentinel said. Not an introduction, a designation. An acknowledgment of what she was in this context.

Avril looked at her. "July 7th," he said.

She didn't answer immediately. She looked at the grimy window for a moment, at the flat light coming through it, and then back at him. "There were fourteen of us in the room that night," she said. "I've thought about all fourteen of us a great deal since then. What we chose and what we didn't. The ones who stayed and the ones who didn't." A pause. "I stayed. I told myself it was to watch. To document. That's what SABLE_VERITY told herself, too. I don't think it was entirely a lie. But it was also easier than leaving."

"You triggered the flare," Avril said.

"Yes."

"That was not easier."

She looked at him steadily. "No," she said. "It wasn't."

Grey Sentinel had been standing against the wall with the particular quality of a man who had said everything he needed to say to get them to this room and was now content to let the room do the work. He spoke now, once. "She has the name."

HARBOR reached into the inside pocket of her jacket and placed a folded piece of paper on the desk between them. She did not unfold it.

"I've been carrying this for three weeks," she said. "I didn't transmit it because there is no channel through which transmitting this name is safe. Not because of what it would expose, but because of who monitors every channel ever associated with this work. Including yours."

"NOMAD," Avril said.

"NOMAD is the mechanism. The person is something else." She looked at the folded paper. "The name on that paper has held a position inside the current operating apparatus of the United States government for nine years. Before that, seven years in a predecessor entity. Before that, she was an operational architect for Directorate Eleven's second phase, which began in 1994. She has been continuous. Everything else around her has changed: administrations, designations, oversight structures, chains of command. She has been continuous."

Avril unfolded the paper.

He read the name. He read it again.

He had seen it before. Not in the Tower Sentinel documentation, not in the targeting criteria, not in the NOMAD budget line, though Daniels would find it in all three when he ran it. He had seen it in the network's early months, in a briefing summary that had passed through his hands before he understood what he was building and the kind of attention it would attract. A name in a position of institutional authority that had seemed, at the time, too senior to be specifically concerned with something as small as We Resist.

It had not been too senior. It had been the origin.

He folded the paper. He put it in his jacket.

HARBOR was watching him. "She knows about this meeting," she said. "Not the specifics. The general shape. She's been watching Grey Sentinel for eight months. She's been watching you for longer."

"How long?" Carrick said. It was the first thing he had said in the room.

HARBOR looked at him. "Before the network launched. Before you decided to build it." She said the last sentence with the weight of someone quoting something they had considered carefully. "That's the phrase I came to use. Before you decide. The decision was what she was waiting for. Not the network, the decision."

The room held that.

"What do you want?" Avril said.

"I want the same thing SABLE_VERITY wants," she said. "For the documentation to become a case. For the case to become a fact in the world that can't be unwritten." She stood. "I can't give you more than the name. But the name, with everything else you have, should be enough."

"Should be," Carrick said.

"Should be," she agreed. She picked up her coat. "Get your journalist free. That's the next thing. Everything else follows from that."

She left without looking back. Grey Sentinel followed her, pausing at the door long enough to say, "I won't be on any channel after today. Whatever comes next, you're carrying it."

Then he was gone too. The door settled. The flat light came through the grimy window.

Carrick and Avril stood in the room for a moment.

"She was right about the monitoring," Carrick said. "If the name comes back clean in the documentation, that confirms it. But it also means the person has been reading our work the same way we've been doing hers."

"I know," Avril said.

"Then she knows we have the name now."

"Yes."

Carrick looked at the window. "Then the clock is different from what it was this morning."

"Yes," Avril said. "It is. Let's go."

He sent the name to Daniels before they left the city. Two hours later, driving back through the kind of flat midwinter landscape that offered nothing to the eye but distance, his phone, the clean one, the one Daniels used only when the channel had been confirmed empty, vibrated once.

The message was four lines.

"NAME CONFIRMED IN TOWER SENTINEL OPERATIONAL RECORDS: AUTHORISING OFFICER, PHASE 2.

NAME CONFIRMED IN NOMAD BUDGET LINE: PROGRAM ARCHITECT, INCEPTION THROUGH YEAR 12.

NAME CONFIRMED IN TARGETING CRITERIA DOCUMENT: SIGNATORY, DOMESTIC IMPLEMENTATION DIRECTIVE.

SHE SIGNED THE ORDER THAT FLAGGED LINA ALVAREZ."

Avril read it once. He didn't read it again. He put the phone away and looked at the road.

Carrick drove without speaking for a long time. Then, "The targeting criteria. She signed the order."

"Yes."

"That makes it personal."

"It's always been personal," Avril said. "Now it's also traceable."

The team assembled around the table that evening. Daniels had the documentation cross-references laid out, three separate threads, each confirming the same name, the paper trail that ran from a domestic implementation directive through a NOMAD inception budget through a Tower Sentinel authorisation, all to the same signature.

Eliana read it carefully and then set it down. "We have the name. We have the documentation connecting her to all three programs. We have HARBOR's testimony, for whatever it's worth, without a formal proceeding. And we have a verified case that Trina built and that Trina is currently prevented from presenting."

"So we have everything except the person who can make it matter," Reyes said.

"We have everything except two things," Eliana said. "Trina, and a venue." She looked at Avril. "A name is not a case. A name attached to documentation that no one can present in a credible public forum is just intelligence. It's useful. But it's not enough."

"HARBOR said get Trina free," Mason said. "That's the next thing."

"HARBOR also said the person who signed the targeting directive knows we have the name," Carrick said. "Which means she knows what we have, and she knows that Trina is the difference between what we have being a case and what we have being noise." He paused. "She'll move on, Trina, before we can."

The room was quiet.

"How long?" Avril said.

"Hours," Carrick said. "Not days. If she were watching the channel that sent the name, she would know the meeting happened. She knows what changed today."

"Then we move tonight," Avril said.

"We don't have a plan for tonight," Reyes said.

"We have the structure of one," Avril said. "Trina isn't in a facility. The NSA Advisor put her in a protected witness category, which means she's accessible through institutional channels. We need someone who can reach her through those channels before whoever is moving against her does."

The room considered what that meant. It meant the network's ability to reach Trina depended entirely on a person they had never met and had no direct contact with, the NSA Advisor, who had been tracing the same thread from the other end, had committed five unauthorized acts without the institution's knowledge, and had just received a response from inside Directorate Eleven that she hadn't yet acted on.

"We can't reach her," Mason said.

"SABLE_VERITY can," Avril said. "HARBOR reached us through SABLE_VERITY's channel. The NSA Advisor sent her transmission through an old channel that HARBOR was monitoring. SABLE_VERITY is the connection between the two."

He looked at Mason. "Ask SABLE_VERITY to reach HARBOR. Tell HARBOR the name is confirmed, and the clock is now. She'll know what to do."

"You're trusting someone you met once," Eliana said.

"I'm trusting someone who pulled a flare gun in a room full of people who didn't," Avril said. "Thirty years ago. That's a long time to stay consistent."

Eliana looked at him for a moment. Then she nodded, the nod of someone who had asked the hard question and received an answer that wasn't comfortable but was sufficient.

He found her in the same place he always found her when the day had been what this day had been: the kitchen table, the atlas, the particular quality of stillness that was not waiting but had become indistinguishable from it.

The atlas was open to the Honduras page. The star was still there in her daughter's pencil, "papi" in careful child's letters, and the page had been handled enough times now that it was slightly softened at the edges, the way pages got when they had been turned to often.

He sat down.

He didn't tell her about the name. He didn't tell her about the meeting, HARBOR, or what Daniels had found in the targeting criteria. He had learned, over the months she had been in the building, that the things he withheld from Naomi weren't the things she needed protection from; she had already been inside the machine's version of what happened to people who knew too much, but the things that weren't yet facts. The name was a fact. Carrick's assessment of the timeline was a fact. What followed from both wasn't yet.

"Reyes has a window," he said. "Small. Two days, maybe three. He's confirming it."

Something shifted in her face, not hope, because she had learned to hold that at a distance, but the particular adjustment of someone who has been accounting for an absence and has just been told the account might be closing.

"Two days," she said.

"Maybe three."

She looked at the star on the Honduras page. Her daughter had added something since yesterday, a small line extending from the star toward the coast, with an arrow at the end pointing toward the sea—the logic of a child who understood departure better than she should have.

"She said he'd go to the water when he got out," Naomi said. "She said he always talked about the Atlantic."

Avril looked at the arrow. He thought about the name in his jacket pocket, folded beside the scarf that had no scent left. The person who had signed the order flagging a civics teacher in a twenty-three-second video had signed it thirty-one years into a career, building the conditions that made resistance impossible before it could begin. And here were the atlas, the star, and the arrow toward the sea, drawn by a child who had learned to map the distance between where things were and where they were supposed to be.

"She's right," he said. "About the water."

Naomi looked at him with the particular attention she gave things that mattered. She didn't ask what he meant. She understood he was talking about more than Carlos, and she let that understanding sit between them without requiring it to become a sentence.

He left her there with the atlas. He went to find Mason.

The message to SABLE_VERITY was six words: "CLOCK IS NOW. HARBOR KNOWS WHAT TO DO."

He sent it. Then he sat and waited for the answer that would tell him whether the last piece would hold.

Chapter Twenty-Four: The Clock

The request came through location designation 7 at 0740. She had noted the designation eleven days ago and had not acted on it. That was a decision rather than an omission. She had been waiting to understand what kind of contact would use it before deciding what kind of contact she was willing to be.

HARBOR had used it. The request was four sentences. It named Trina Cole, named the current classification, named the authority under which a reclassification could be made, and named what the reclassification needed to produce: accessibility by legal counsel initiated within the protected witness framework, without generating a flag on the systems that monitored protected witness movements.

It was the smallest possible action. It was also precisely targeted. Whoever had drafted it understood the institutional architecture well enough to know exactly which lever produced the needed result without touching anything adjacent. That kind of precision was either the work of someone who had spent years inside the apparatus or someone who had been briefed by someone who had.

She read it twice. Then she opened the relevant system, made the reclassification through an authority she technically held and had not previously used, and closed the system. Twelve minutes start to finish. She did not log her reasoning. There was no field for reasoning in the relevant form, which she had always found to be one of its more useful features.

She went back to the work on her desk. It was a Tuesday. The day continued as Tuesdays did.

She had now done six things the institution did not know she had done. She had stopped counting them as a way of managing the weight and started counting them as a way of being precise about what she had committed to. Six things, each one smaller than it would have needed to be if the ones before it had not happened. That was how it worked when you did things carefully. Each action made the next one more specific, the way a path through a field became more defined the more people walked it, until it was no longer a choice but a route.

He found it at 1130, running the monitoring thread he had been maintaining since the NSA Advisor placed Trina in the protected witness category. Not a breach, not a flag, a reclassification processed through the correct authority, generating no alert. The kind of movement that the system treated as routine because it had been executed correctly.

He sat with it for a few minutes. The reclassification made Trina reachable by her own legal counsel through the protected witness framework, a narrow channel but a real one. Whoever had done it had known how to do it in a way that did not draw attention. That kind of knowledge had a specific profile.

He went to find Avril.

"Trina's classification shifted this morning," he said. "She's reachable. Someone with the right institutional authority made the change through the correct channel. No flag, no alert. Whoever did it knew what they were doing."

Avril read the notation Daniels handed him. He was quiet for a moment.

"Legal counsel can reach her," Daniels said. "Through the protected witness channel. It's narrow, but it's there."

"Yes," Avril said.

Daniels waited. He understood from the quality of Avril's silence that Avril knew more about the mechanism than he was going to say, and that not saying it was itself information. "I'll keep monitoring the channel," he said.

"Yes," Avril said. "Thank you."

Daniels left. Avril sat with the notation for a while, thinking about HARBOR and the twelve minutes it had taken someone to do what the network had taken eleven months to approach. He thought about what it meant to have the right credential and the right position and the willingness to use both in a way that could not be undone. He thought about the six things the NSA Advisor had done, the last of which had just made Trina Cole accessible, and whether she knew that the person she had just helped was the journalist whose verification was the difference between a name in his jacket pocket being intelligence and being a case.

She did not know. The two investigations had converged on the same point from opposite ends and still had not met. Whatever came next, they were carrying it separately.

He came to Avril that afternoon with the particular economy of movement that meant he had been ready for longer than the conversation would suggest.

"Two days," he said. "The facility runs a contractor oversight rotation on a seventy-two-hour cycle. There's a gap in the overlap, a four-hour window where the secondary oversight tier is not active. It's not a hole in the security, it's an administrative gap. They know it exists. They've accepted it because the gap has never been exploited."

"Until now," Avril said.

"Carlos is in the same block he's been in since the transfer. I've confirmed it through two separate source threads in the last week." Reyes set a single page on the table, a hand-drawn floor map from someone who had worked from multiple partial sources and triangulated. "Ingress through the service corridor. The same contractor structure as CSI-7, same parent company, same badge architecture. The identity packet we used there should work with modifications."

"Soto drives," Avril said.

"Soto drives." Reyes paused. "I need Carrick on the exterior. And I need a decision now, because the window opens in forty hours and the preparation takes thirty."

Avril looked at the map. He looked at the window notation, four hours, administrative gap, never exploited. He thought about the ten months Carlos Ellis had been in a facility operating under a contractor structure built by the same entity that had built CSI-7, which had been built by the same entity whose budget line traced back to NOMAD, which had been built to serve Directorate Eleven. The machine was coherent all the way down. That coherence was also a vulnerability. Once you understood the architecture, the gaps were predictable.

"Yes," he said. "Go."

Reyes nodded and picked up the map. He was already somewhere else in his mind, the service corridor, the badge reader, the forty hours of preparation that would look from the outside like nothing at all.

Eliana found Naomi at the kitchen table with the atlas open, which was where Naomi was most afternoons now. The Honduras page. The star in her daughter's pencil. The arrow toward the sea.

She sat down across from her without preamble, which was the register Naomi had made clear she preferred, not by saying so, but by the quality of attention she gave to people who did not soften things before saying them.

"Reyes has a window," Eliana said. "Forty hours. He's moving."

Naomi looked at her with the stillness she had developed over ten months of waiting, not the stillness of someone who had given up, but of someone who had learned to hold things at a temperature that did not consume them. "He's still there," she said.

"Yes," Eliana said.

Naomi nodded. She looked down at the atlas, at the star, at the arrow, at the capital city her daughter had labeled in careful handwriting. Then she closed it. She set her hand flat on the cover for a long time, not dramatically, just the way you kept your hand on a door after you closed it to make sure it had caught. Eliana watched and said nothing.

Later, Naomi's daughter asked where the atlas was.

Naomi said, "It's put away for now."

Her daughter accepted this with the equanimity of a child who had learned that things being put away was sometimes a form of respect for them. She went back to what she had been doing.

That night, for the first time in as long as Eliana could remember, the safehouse was quiet in a different way than usual, not the quiet of people managing tension, but the quiet of people waiting for something they had been told was coming.

He sat at the table after the house had gone quiet. The paper with the name on it was in his jacket pocket. The scarf was beside him on the table. He had stopped carrying it folded and had started setting it down in front of him when he needed to think, the way some people kept objects on their desks that had no function except to be held.

There was nothing left to smell. The cedar and ink had been gone for weeks. What remained was the shape of it, the weight, the fact that it had been Lena's and was now his and would eventually be nothing recognizable at all. He had not decided what to do with it when it reached that point. He was not ready to decide.

He thought about what HARBOR had said in the insurance archive building, in the flat gray light. "Get your journalist free. That's the next thing. Everything else follows from that." He thought about the twelve minutes it had taken someone to do what eleven months of careful work had been building toward. He thought about Trina Cole in whatever room she was in, now reachable, with the flash drive and the targeting criteria and the treaty compliance files and the verified connection between all three and the name he was carrying.

Two days for the window at Waverly. Less than that before Trina's legal counsel could reach her through the reclassified channel.

Both things moving in the same forty-eight hours without coordination, because the threads had run to the length where they resolved or they broke. He had not planned for them to converge here. He had planned each one carefully and separately, and they had converged anyway, which was either very good or the kind of coincidence that the machine was built to exploit. He did not know which.

He picked up the scarf. He held it for a moment. Then he folded it and put it back in his jacket pocket, next to the name.

From the other room, Mason was running a check, the flat functional sounds of the work that continued as long as the network continued. From somewhere further in the building, the low sound of Naomi's daughter asking Eliana something, and Eliana's voice answering, patient, precise, the same register she used for everything that mattered.

He opened the notebook. He wrote the date. He wrote: TRINA REACHABLE. WAVERLY WINDOW: 40 HRS. CLOCK IS NOW.

He closed the notebook and left it on the table.

Then he went to find Carrick, because there was work to do and thirty hours was not a long time.

Chapter Twenty-Five: Waverly

Tennessee in late winter had a particular quality of flatness, not the flatness of absence but of things waiting. The fields ran to the horizon without drama. The sky was the color of paper left too long in a window. The road to Waverly was the kind of road that existed to connect two places neither of which was a destination.

Soto drove. He had been driving since before dawn, which he had done without complaint and without comment, because driving was what Soto did and he did it the way he did everything, precisely, without performance. He parked where Reyes indicated, a service access road two hundred meters from the facility's secondary perimeter, screened from the main approach by a stand of bare trees that would offer better cover in six weeks but offered enough now.

The facility looked like what it was pretending to be, a regional administrative processing center operated by a contractor whose parent company had a parent company whose parent company traced back to the same procurement chain as CSI-7 and the Pennsylvania site. The same architecture, corporate placards, security cameras calibrated for deterrence rather than detection, a light guard presence designed to suggest that nothing inside required heavy guarding. Reyes had read all of this from the documents Daniels had pulled three weeks ago and had been reading it again in the approach, checking his understanding against the building in front of him.

"Badge reader on the service entrance is the same model as Pennsylvania," he said. "It responds to the packet on the second ping. Do not rush the first."

Carrick was already out of the van, moving toward the exterior position he had identified from the aerial map. He did not acknowledge this because he already knew it. That was the quality of their work at this point. The briefings had become confirmation rather than instruction.

Reyes checked the modified identity packet one more time. Then he walked toward the service entrance, unhurried, the way you walked toward a door you expected to open.

The badge reader responded on the second ping. The corridor inside was colder than the exterior, which Reyes had expected. The same climate logic as CSI-7, discomfort as a management tool. The floor plan Daniels had sourced showed a direct route to the detention block, but the direct route required passing through a checkpoint that was not on the floor plan, which meant the floor plan was eight months old and the facility had been modified.

Reyes stopped. He looked at the checkpoint, a desk, one guard, a scanner, then at the corridor to the left, which was not on the floor plan either but which led by the logic of the building's structure toward the same destination by a longer path.

He took the longer path.

It added four minutes. At the three-minute mark, Carrick's voice came through the comm bead, one click, which meant the exterior was clean. At the four-minute mark, Reyes reached the detention block and found it arranged exactly as the floor plan showed, which meant the modifications were confined to the front half of the building. The contractor had added a checkpoint without updating the documentation it provided to oversight bodies, which was either incompetence or the kind of deliberate opacity that the oversight bodies had learned not to look for.

Carlos Ellis was in the third cell of the second row. The cell designation matched what Reyes had confirmed through two source threads over the previous week. He was sitting on the edge of the cot when Reyes opened the door, sitting upright, the way someone sat when they had been sitting upright for a long time and had stopped noticing they were doing it.

He looked at Reyes. He had the particular quality of attention of someone who had learned that the appearance of guards in doorways was rarely good and was recalibrating this appearance against that expectation.

"Your wife sent us," Reyes said. "Your daughter too. We need to go now."

Carlos Ellis stood up. He was wearing the facility's gray clothing, which he left on because there was not time to change and because Reyes had a maintenance jacket in the bag over his shoulder that was the more important layer. He put on the jacket without being asked. He had, Reyes noted, the kind of practical intelligence that did not require things to be explained twice.

They went.

The longer path back was the same four minutes in reverse, with the difference that two people moving through a corridor read differently than one. Reyes set the pace. Carlos matched it, shoulders down, eyes forward, the posture of someone who had been in enough institutional spaces to understand that the way you moved through them was itself a form of identification.

At the junction before the service entrance, a guard appeared from a side corridor. Not the checkpoint guard, a different one, doing a circuit that the floor plan had not shown because it was a roving pattern rather than a fixed post. He looked at them with the unfocused attention of someone two hours into a shift that offered nothing to focus on.

Reyes handed him the work order from the top of the folder, a single sheet, the kind that existed to be handed to people and not read carefully. "Fiber check on the east conduit," he said. "We are on our way out."

The guard looked at the sheet. He looked at Carlos. Carlos was looking at a point slightly above and to the left of the guard's head, which was the correct place to look.

"Sign out at the desk," the guard said.

"Already done," Reyes said. "Electronic log, fifteen minutes ago."

The guard nodded without checking this because checking it would require a radio call that would interrupt his circuit, and the circuit was the thing his shift evaluation was based on. He moved on. Reyes and Carlos moved on. The service entrance was twenty meters ahead.

The badge reader released the door on the first ping this time, which was either a different calibration on the exit side or a coincidence. Reyes did not pause to consider which.

They walked to the van. Soto had the engine running.

Carrick was already in the front when they reached the van. He looked at Carlos once, the comprehensive look he gave to new variables in his vicinity, then looked back at the road ahead, which Soto was already navigating.

They drove for twenty minutes in silence before Carlos spoke.

"My family," he said. "Are they…"

"Safe," Reyes said. "They have been safe for months."

Carlos absorbed this the way you absorbed information that you had been trying not to need. He looked out the window at the Tennessee flatness running past.

"My daughter," he asked. "Is she…"

"She has been working on an atlas," Reyes said. "Geography. She knows a lot about Central America now."

Carlos looked at him. Something shifted in his face, not quite a smile, not quite anything else. He turned back to the window.

He slept an hour outside Nashville. He slept the way people slept when they had been rationing sleep for a long time and had just been given permission to stop, not gradually but all at once, the body making a decision the mind did not have time to supervize. Reyes watched the road. Soto drove. Carrick did whatever Carrick did when he had nothing to do, which looked from the outside like nothing but was probably several things.

The drive was four hours. It was ordinary in the way that things were ordinary when the extraordinary thing had already happened and what remained was just the distance between it and the next moment.

He heard the van first, the specific sound of Soto's approach, which he had learned to distinguish over many months from other vehicles on the road outside. He was in the hallway when the door opened.

Naomi's daughter heard it before any of them. She had been in the back room and came through the hallway at a speed that suggested she had been waiting for that specific sound for longer than anyone had told her to. She passed Avril without seeing him. She went through the door.

He heard her voice. He heard Naomi's voice behind her, lower, the voice of someone who had been holding something at a specific temperature for ten months and was only now allowing the temperature to change. He heard a third voice, a man's voice, the register of someone speaking quietly in a language he understood but that was not the language of this building, and then sounds that were not voices, a chair, movement, the particular acoustic signature of people in a small room who had collapsed the distance between them.

Avril stayed in the hallway. He put his back against the wall and stood there.

He was not part of what was happening in that room. He was adjacent to it, which was the correct position. He had spent ten months moving people toward reunions he would not attend, building chains of custody for evidence he would not present, documenting things he would not be able to publicly confirm. The hallway was the logical conclusion of that work. He was in it, the room was full, and those were not the same thing.

He stayed until the sounds settled into something quieter, the particular quiet of people who had stopped needing to speak because speaking was no longer the most efficient way to be present. Then he went back to the kitchen and sat down at the table.

She came to find him an hour later, maybe two. He had made coffee and drunk it and made more. The house had the quality of a place that had changed register without changing anything visible.

Naomi sat down across from him. She did not speak for a moment, which was consistent with how she had been since Louisville, the particular economy of someone who had learned that words were a resource and should be spent accordingly.

Then she reached across the table and picked up the atlas, which her daughter had left there, the Honduras page still marked with the receipt strip, the star in pencil, the arrow toward the sea.

She opened it. She looked at the star and the arrow for a moment. She picked up the pencil her daughter had left on the table and drew a small line from the tip of the arrow back to the star, a return, a completion of the circuit the arrow had implied. She set the pencil down.

She closed the atlas. She stood up and put it on the shelf above the table, spine out, the way you shelved a book you had finished reading and wanted to keep.

She went back to the other room without speaking. He did not need her to.

He sat at the table until the light changed. The house was making sounds it had not made before, a low voice from the back, the sound of water running, something that might have been laughter and might not have been, the ordinary noise of people in a building being people.

He opened the notebook. He looked at what he had written the night before. TRINA REACHABLE. WAVERLY WINDOW: 40

HRS. CLOCK IS NOW. He drew a single line through it, not to erase it, just to mark it as a thing that had happened. Then he turned to a fresh page and looked at it for a while without writing anything.

There was still work. Trina, and the case, and the name in his pocket, and everything that followed from the name being in his pocket. The chapter he was in now was not the last chapter. But it was the one that had required ten months of other chapters to reach, and he was in no hurry to leave it.

He thought about Lina Alvarez. Twenty-seven, civics teacher. The van doors. The twenty-three seconds. He thought about the arrow on the Honduras page and the line drawn back to the star and the atlas on the shelf, finished. He thought about what it meant that one family was in a room in this building right now because the documentation had held, the chain of custody had held, the people had held, not without cost, not without loss, but held.

He thought about all the families that had not.

Then he got up and made coffee, because the day was starting and the next thing was already waiting, and the only thing to do with the next thing was to begin it.

Chapter Twenty-Six: Trina

She had been in rooms that were not her own for long enough that she had stopped grieving the distinction. This one had a window that faced east, which meant the light came in the morning and left by early afternoon. She had organized her work around that: the reading in the morning, the writing when the light was still good, the verification checks in the evening when the room went gray, and the screen was easier to look at than the window.

The legal counsel had reached her three weeks after the reclassification. Three meetings, careful, everything through the correct channel. She had not asked how the reclassification happened. She understood from the quality of her counsel's caution that the answer to that question was not something either of them should be holding.

What she held instead was the documentation. She had been holding it since the locker at the transit hub, the flash drive, the targeting criteria document that had arrived through the verified channel weeks before that, the treaty compliance files she had been working with since the beginning. She had read all of it carefully, in the order that made the connections legible, and she had written the chain of custody document that described each piece, its provenance, the verification steps she had applied, and the cross references that connected them.

The chain of custody was longer than the documentation itself. That was intentional. The documentation proved what happened. The chain of custody proved that the documentation proved it.

There were names on the targeting criteria list. She had decided early not to read them individually. She understood that the list contained people, that each entry was a person flagged by a program designed to flag people like them, and that some of those people had lost things she could not restore through any filing. But she had also understood that reading the names would change the quality of her attention in ways that would make the work harder to do correctly. She needed precision. Precision required distance from the weight of things, and she had maintained that distance for eleven months. The names were in the filing now, and she still did not know them.

She had thought, occasionally, about whether that was a failure. She had decided it was not. It was a method. What would have been a failure was doing the work badly because she had let the weight of it sit in the wrong part of her.

The decision about where to file had taken longer than the documentation itself.

A journalist was a single point of failure. She had seen a single point of failure used once already, the documentation released without provenance, the verification chain stripped, the truth made available in a form designed to make it unprovable. A journalist, even a careful one, was one person who could be pressured, whose publication could be acquired, whose editors could make decisions she had no control over. She ruled that out.

A congressional submission was too slow and too visible. The machinery would absorb it. It would become a footnote in a process designed to produce footnotes.

What she chose instead took two weeks to research and three days to confirm was still viable. A federal civil liberties case currently in the fourth circuit, already in discovery, already generating a record, had a filing window that would accept the documentation as an exhibit if submitted with a verified chain of custody and a declaration of provenance. The documentation would become part of an existing legal record. It would be indexed. It would be searchable. It would be there the next time a judge asked for verification of a detention list and refused to proceed without it.

The second submission was to a legal evidence archive at a law school that had been preserving records since the COINTELPRO era. They had a submission protocol for exactly this category of material. The protocol was unglamorous and thorough, a verification process that would take weeks, during which the documentation would sit in a holding queue behind forty years of similar material, and at the end of which it would be cataloged and preserved in a form still accessible in thirty years.

The third was a copy to a second law school, different jurisdiction, different archive, same verification standard. Redundancy. She had learned from the flash drive and from everything before it that single copies of things were not preservation. Preservation was distribution to enough places that the loss of any one of them did not matter.

She began the filing at nine in the morning, when the light was good.

The federal court submission first. She had the case number, the filing window, the declaration of provenance she had written and rewritten until the language was precisely what the court's submission guidelines required, no more and no less. She attached the documentation in the specified format. She attached the chain of custody document. She generated the hash verification for each file and recorded it in the submission log. She submitted it through the court's electronic filing system, which issued a confirmation number. She wrote it in her notebook next to the date and time.

The law school archive second. Different system, different format requirements, the same documentation prepared differently for a different context. The submission protocol required her to complete a provenance declaration that asked how the material had come into her possession. She answered carefully, accurately, and with the specific omissions her legal counsel had advised were both permissible and prudent. The system accepted the submission and generated a queue confirmation. She wrote the number in her notebook.

The second law school third. By now the work had the quality of repetition she associated with things done correctly, not monotonous, but settled, each step building on the verification of the step before it. She submitted. She received a confirmation. She wrote it down.

She looked at the notebook. Three confirmation numbers, three timestamps, the date.

Then she closed the laptop.

She filled the kettle from the tap and set it on the burner and stood at the window while it heated. The light had moved while she worked. It was past noon now, the direct sun gone, the room in flat indirect light that meant the afternoon had started without her noticing.

She thought about the chain of custody document. Twenty-three pages. She had written it in the language of legal evidence because that was the language that would make it usable, but what it described was eleven months of other people doing things she had only heard about at a distance, a flash drive passed through a dental crown, a locker in a transit hub, a verified channel accessed through a device she no longer had. People she had never met doing work she could not fully account for because they had decided the documentation was worth the cost of the work. She had been, for most of that time, a destination. A place the material was traveling toward.

The kettle boiled. She made the tea, the specific sequence of it, the timing, the temperature she preferred, and she carried the mug to the chair by the window and sat down.

The room was quiet. Outside, whatever was outside, the ordinary sounds of a street in the middle of the day, people going somewhere, the acoustic texture of a city that did not know what had just been filed in its courts and its archives and would not know for a long time. Maybe for years. Maybe longer.

She drank the tea.

The documentation was in three places now, and it would be there tomorrow, and the filing confirmation numbers were in her notebook, and she was a person sitting in a chair by a window in a room that was not her own, and the thing she had been carrying for eleven months was not gone. It was still in the record. It would always be in the record. But it was no longer only in her hands.

That was what she had been working toward. Not the filing itself. The moment after it, when the weight redistributed, when she was still holding it but no longer the only one.

She sat there for a while. The light stayed flat and even. She finished the tea. She did not open the laptop again.

Chapter Twenty-Seven: The Name in the Archive

The brief was three pages. It had been written by someone two levels below her who understood the situation accurately and was trying to characterize it in language she would find useful, which was the brief's only ambition and which it achieved.

The first page described the filing: a federal civil liberties case in the Fourth Circuit, documentary exhibit submitted with a verified chain of custody, cross-referencing Tower Sentinel operational records, a domestic targeting program designated NOMAD, and a budget line that traced through a series of absorbed entities to a current operating unit. The exhibit is named the unit. The exhibit is named the program architect.

The second page described the distribution: two law school evidence archives in different jurisdictions with the same verification standard. The documentation indexed, cataloged, preserved. Searchable. The brief used the word searchable once, in the second paragraph of the second page, with the emphasis of someone who understood that this was the operative fact.

The third page contained the recommendation.

She read the brief at her desk on a Tuesday morning. She had been at this desk, in variations of this position, for nine years in the current role. Before that, seven years in the predecessor entity. Before that, the years she did not account for publicly, doing the work that had produced the conditions for everything that came after.

The recommendation was accurate. She understood this immediately, the way she understood most things that arrived in the form of a correctly reasoned brief, not because she agreed with the conclusion, but because the logic was sound and the conclusion followed from the logic and the logic was based on facts that were now fixed.

The documentation was in three repositories and a federal court record. Pursuit of the individuals who had assembled it would make the documentation more visible without making it less true. The phenomenon had, as the brief correctly stated, decoupled from its leadership. There was no longer a leadership to pursue. There was a record.

She closed the folder.

She did not issue a counter directive. There was no counter directive that would change the facts the brief described. The machine did not reverse, it adjusted. It learned, as it had always learned, what it could no longer usefully do, and filed that learning in the part of itself that would apply it next time.

She put the folder in the drawer. She went back to the work on her desk, which was the work of the current day and did not require her to think about this further.

She did not think about it further.

He found it on a Thursday, running a cross-reference check he had been running weekly since the documentation was assembled, a search against public legal databases for any record that matched the hash signatures of the materials he had traced internally. He had been running it for six weeks without a result. On the seventh week the result came back.

He looked at it for a long time before he printed it.

The filing was an exhibit in a civil liberties case in the fourth circuit. The exhibit was sixty-three pages: the documentation itself, the hash verification for each component, and a chain of custody document that described the provenance of every piece of material, the verification steps applied to each, and the cross-references that connected them. The chain of custody was twenty-three pages. He read it carefully, the way he read things that required precision rather than speed.

The verification methodology was the same methodology he had been using. The same standards, the same cross-referencing structure, the same approach to establishing provenance through adjacent records when the primary record was inaccessible. He had developed his methodology independently, working from the inside. Whoever had built this chain of custody had developed theirs independently, working from the outside. They had arrived at the same place.

He read the declaration of provenance at the end of the chain of custody document. It named the verifying journalist. He had not known this name before.

He printed the filing and took it to Avril.

Avril was at the table when Daniels came in. He had been there most of the morning, not working exactly, but present in the way you were present when you were waiting for the shape of something to become clear.

Daniels set the printout on the table without preamble. "Federal civil liberties case, Fourth Circuit. Documentary exhibit, filed six days ago. Chain of custody, twenty-three pages. The documentation matches everything we've traced. Tower Sentinel, NOMAD, the targeting criteria, the budget line." He paused. "The name is in the exhibit. Searchable."

Avril looked at the printout. He looked at the confirmation numbers at the top of the chain of custody document, three of them, three different repositories, the timestamps six days earlier.

"The journalist," Daniels said. "The chain of custody names her." He looked at the page. "Trina Cole."

Avril was quiet. Not a moment longer than a moment. He looked at the name in the document the way you looked at something you had been carrying toward without knowing that was what you were doing, and had now arrived at, and the arrival was not what you had imagined because you had never let yourself imagine it clearly enough to be wrong about it.

He had known her name for months. He had known what she was building. He had not known, until this sentence, that the building was complete.

He read the name again. In the document, in Daniels' voice, in the chain of custody that had been eleven months in the making and was now a public exhibit in a federal court record. The same name. Different weight.

"She did this alone," he said. Not a question.

"The chain of custody covers eleven months of verification work," Daniels said. "Whatever access she had to the source materials, she built the methodology herself. From the outside." He paused. "The verification standard is the same as ours. I don't know if she knew that."

"She didn't," Avril said. "We didn't know about each other."

He picked up the printout and read through the chain of custody document slowly. The flash drive. The targeting criteria document. The treaty compliance files. Each one sourced, verified, cross-referenced, its provenance established through the exact sequence of adjacent records that he had been tracing from the other direction. Two people who had never met, working toward the same point from opposite ends, using the same method without knowing it.

He set the printout down.

"The name," he said. "It's in the exhibit?"

"In the targeting criteria document, which is now a public exhibit," Daniels said. "Searchable by anyone running a cross-reference on the unit designation. She's still in her position. There's no proceeding. The documentation doesn't produce accountability, it produces a record."

Avril looked at the printout. He had known this. He had understood it since the early months, when he had first built We Resist and understood that documentation was not justice, that the record surviving was a different thing from the record mattering, that the distance between a thing being provable and a thing being proven was the whole distance between where they were and where they needed to be.

He had known it and he had built the archive anyway. He had built it because the record was what was possible to build, and because the record would be there when, if, the other things became possible, and because the alternative was leaving people in a system that had decided they did not exist.

"Yes," he said. "That's what it produces."

Daniels nodded. He understood, from the quality of the silence, that this was not a small thing to say. He picked up his copy of the printout and went back to work.

The sounds of the building settled around Avril, Mason at the monitoring station, the specific quality of a house in the middle of the afternoon, the ordinary ongoing texture of people doing things in rooms.

He sat with it for a long time.

He thought about the things that had to hold for the printout to exist on the table in front of him. SABLE_VERITY's decision to leave the apparatus and keep the documentation. The targeting criteria document was held for three years by a man in a gray coat in an abandoned seminary. HARBOR in a room on July 7th, pulling a flare. Grey Sentinel across four relay hops on a ghost frequency, not coming back. The NSA Advisor's twelve minutes and the form with no field for reasoning. Reyes at Waverly, the longer corridor, the work order, thirty seconds of patience. The chain of custody Claire had carried in a dental crown to a room he had never been in, and that Trina had spent eleven months turning into twenty-three pages that would now live in the fourth circuit record indefinitely.

All of it pointing toward a printout on a table in an ordinary room on a Thursday afternoon, with Daniels' handwriting in the margin noting the date he had found it.

He reached into his jacket and took out the scarf. There was very little left of it now. The fabric had thinned at the folds, the color gone flat, the shape it had held for months finally releasing. Cedar and ink had been gone for weeks. What remained was the fact of it. That it had been Lena's, that she had been wearing it, that twenty-three seconds of video had been the thing that made him understand documentation mattered.

He thought about Lina Alvarez. Her name was in the targeting criteria document that was now a public exhibit in a federal civil liberties case. A judge running a cross-reference on the unit designation would find it. A clerk verifying a detention list might find it. A graduate student a year from now would find it.

She was not free. The documentation of what was done to her was in the record. He had understood months ago that those were different things. He understood it again now, sitting with the printout on the table, and it was still true, and still not enough, and still the thing that had been possible to do.

He folded the scarf. He put it back in his jacket. He picked up the printout and put it with the other documents, the notebook, the papers, the record of the months. He sat there until the light changed and the afternoon became evening and Mason called from the other room that there was something on the monitoring thread he should see.

He got up. There was still work. There was always still work. He went to see what Mason had found.

Chapter Twenty-Eight: Dispersal

Mason closed the monitoring station in the order that made sense technically. Active feeds first, the relay monitors, the cascade trackers, the threat flag queue he had been running since Chapter 13 with one brief interruption when the system was compromised and he had to rebuild it from a cold backup. Then the passive monitors, the ones that ran in the background of everything else and produced their quiet data without requiring him to look at it, most of which he had never looked at, all of which had been running. Then the archived relay logs, copied to the secure server that would keep running whether he checked it or not.

He wiped what should be wiped. He preserved what should be preserved. The distinction was technical and he knew it precisely.

When the last terminal went dark, the room lost the particular quality that rooms with running equipment had, a low frequency presence that you stopped noticing until it stopped. He stood in the silence for a moment. Then he turned off the light and left the room, and the room became a room that had not recently been used for anything in particular.

He took nothing with him except the habit of attention, which he had always had and which had been refined by months of watching for signals in noise. It would be useful. He expected it to be useful for the rest of his life, in contexts he could not predict. That seemed like the right kind of thing to take.

He drove them somewhere that was not where they had been and not where they had been before that. Naomi sat in the front seat. The children were in the back, quieter than children usually were on long drives, which he attributed to the particular exhaustion of people who had been in transit for a long time and had learned to rest whenever rest was possible. Carlos was in the back with them. He was asleep before they reached the highway.

Reyes drove. The road was the road. He did not feel the need to fill the drive with conversation, and neither did Naomi, and the silence between them was the silence of two people who understood the same thing about what had just happened and did not need to agree about it out loud.

When they arrived, he helped carry the bags to the door. Naomi said his name once, just his name, nothing following it. He nodded, and that was sufficient for both of them. He got back in the car. He drove back the way he had come.

The atlas was in one of the bags. He knew this because he had seen Naomi pack it. The Honduras page, the star in pencil, the line her daughter had drawn back to the star when Carlos came home. He had not looked at the map closely enough to know if the arrow toward the sea was still there. He thought it was probably. He thought probably the family would find their way to the coast eventually, which was something he had no part in and no need to know about.

He drove. The road went on.

She went back to work. Not the same firm, she had been gone too long, and the firm had redistributed her cases, and going back to redistribute them again would have required explanations she was not prepared to give. A different firm, a different city, the same register, a desk, a case file, the specific language of standing and evidence and what a court will and will not accept.

She was a different person than she had been before Louisville, but she was still a lawyer. The difference was not in the tools. It was in how she understood what the tools were for.

She had learned, in the months of the network's work, that documentation was not passive. That building a chain of custody was an act in the same way that filing an injunction was an act. It produced a fact in the world that had not existed before the act. She had known this technically before. She understood it differently now.

She took one case in the first month that she would not have taken before Louisville. A man whose immigration status had been affected by a surveillance designation she recognized from the targeting criteria documentation now in the federal record. She did not tell him she recognized it. She built the case from the evidence that was available, which was more available than it had been six months ago, because of the filing, because of the archive, because of the chain of custody that someone had spent twenty-three pages building. She did not know who had built it. It did not matter.

She won the case on a Friday afternoon, without ceremony, in the way that most cases were won, by the record being what the record was.

He parked the car. He got out. He walked away from it.

He had been the person who drove, and he had driven well, and the driving was done. He became invisible in the way that people who were always slightly invisible became invisible when they stopped having a reason to be noticed, completely, without effort, as if the visibility had only ever been incidental to a function that was now complete.

The car sat in a parking structure for four days before anyone checked. By then he was somewhere else entirely, doing something ordinary, and no one was looking.

He was the last one in the safehouse. He had not arranged this deliberately, there was no last meeting, no ceremony of ending, no moment when he said something that would require the others to answer. People simply stopped being present, in the way they had gathered, without announcement, in response to the work rather than to a summons.

He walked through the rooms. The monitoring station was a room with a desk and a dark terminal and the absence of the low hum it had been producing for months. The kitchen table had a coffee mug on it and nothing else, and he did not know whose mug it was. The back room where Naomi had been longest was empty in the specific way that rooms were empty after being occupied for a long time, not merely absent of people but full of the shape of their having been there.

He sat at the kitchen table for a while. He was not thinking about anything in particular. He was being somewhere for the last time, which required its own kind of attention and could not be hurried.

Then he picked up the notebook from the table, the same notebook, the one that went back to the beginning, the one with the four facts about the ghost print and the Waverly entry with the line drawn through it and the confirmation numbers from Trina's filing that Daniels had written in the margin, and he put it in his jacket pocket. He stood up.

He took it out for the last time in a room that was not the safehouse, a room he was passing through, a surface he set it on without planning to. He had not planned the moment. It had arrived the way some moments arrived, as a fact rather than a decision.

There was nothing left of it that was the thing it had been. No cedar, no ink, no smell of any kind. The fabric had thinned at every fold until it held its shape only by habit, the shape of being carried, of being taken out and held and put back, repeated so many times that the repetition had become the object's only remaining structure. It was a piece of cloth. It had been Lena's.

He looked at it for a moment, long enough to be honest about what he was looking at and what it had been and what the distance between those two things cost.

Then he looked at the room. The ordinary surfaces of it. The window, the light, the fact of a place that had no particular significance and would have none.

He picked up the notebook. He left the scarf on the surface. It had been Lena's and it had been his and it had been his failure and it had been two years of held distance and one reflex at midnight that he would carry in a different way than he carried everything else, because everything else he had chosen and this he had not been able to stop himself from choosing.

He walked out.

Chapter Twenty-Nine: The Memo

She cleared the morning's work from her desk at half past nine, the briefings, the routing slips, the overnight traffic summary that she had read and annotated and returned to the system. When the desk was clear she took a legal pad from the bottom drawer and set it in front of her. Paper. Not a system.

She dated it. Then she looked at the address line for a moment, because the person she was writing to did not exist yet. The position existed. The office existed. But the individual who would eventually sit at a desk like this one and open an envelope with this classification was not yet knowable. She had to find language for that.

She wrote, "To the occupant of this office, when the materials contained herein become relevant to an active inquiry."

She looked at it. It was accurate. She continued.

She wrote the NOMAD designation first. What it was built to do was persistent monitoring and intervention seeded into infrastructure before resistance movements organized, two native functions, release and observe. She wrote that it had been operational for seventeen years and that its budget line traced through a series of absorbed entities to a current operating unit, and that the unit's name was Directorate Eleven, and that Directorate Eleven had been in continuous operation for thirty years across every administration that had held power during that period.

She wrote that NOMAD was not a surveillance program. She wrote that the distinction mattered. Surveillance programs watched. NOMAD was built to prevent the conditions under which watching became necessary. She wrote, "The system does not monitor resistance. It prevents the infrastructure that resistance requires. It does this by positioning itself inside that infrastructure before it is built."

She paused. She read the sentence back. It was accurate, and she knew it to be accurate, and she had known it since the morning she pulled the classification record through an authentication she was not supposed to have. Saying it in an institutional document with an institutional address was a different kind of knowing from knowing it privately. She had been sitting with the difference for months. Writing it down was the thing that converted one into the other.

She continued.

She wrote the name. Not NOMAD's designation, the person's name. The name that was already in a federal civil liberties exhibit, already searchable by anyone running a cross reference on the unit designation, already in the record. She wrote it here because the record was the record and the institutional document was a different kind of fact, the kind produced by someone with standing, with access, with the specific credential that made the name mean something different in this context than it meant in the archive.

She wrote the three programs she had authorized. She wrote the dates. She wrote the domestic implementation directive and the targeting criteria and the names of the programs that had produced the cases she had been reviewing for the past eleven months, beginning with the cases that had appeared in the channel provenance records and ending with the cases in the federal exhibit filed six weeks ago by a journalist whose name she included because the memo needed the chain of custody, and the chain of custody included that name.

She did not write the network's name. She wrote around it the way you wrote around something you knew was present without wanting to give it a shape that could be used against it in a context you could not anticipate. The network had done what networks did when the work was complete. It had stopped being a network. There was nothing to protect by naming it. There was something to protect by not naming it. She was precise about this.

She wrote the six things she had done. Each one in a numbered paragraph, with the date, the action, the authority she had used or exceeded, and her reasoning. The reasoning was the part she had been composing in her head for months without knowing she was composing it, since the first time she had run a trace on the relay and recognized the architecture, since the first authentication she was not supposed to have, since the twelve minutes she had spent reclassifying a journalist in a protected witness category using a form with no field for reasoning.

The reasoning, written out in full, occupied four pages. She had thought it would be shorter. When she reached the end of the fourth page she read it back from the beginning and found that it was accurate throughout, that every sentence described a decision she had made for the reason she had written, and that the reasons, taken together, described a person who had understood for a long time that the institution she worked for had a function she disagreed with and had continued to work inside it while disagreeing, and had eventually reached the point where continuing to work inside it required her to do things the institution did not know about in order to remain the person she understood herself to be.

She read it back a second time. She did not revise it. She added one sentence at the end of the fourth page: "I would make the same decisions again."

She wrote the recommendations last. They were brief, three paragraphs. The first recommended that whoever opened this envelope cross reference the federal exhibit in the fourth circuit civil liberties case, case number provided, and note that the chain of custody in the exhibit's documentation was independently verifiable through the institutional records she had attached. The second recommended that the NOMAD program designation be treated as an active infrastructure concern rather than a historical one, because the relay architecture persisted and the program's functions would continue to operate until someone with the correct institutional access deactivated them. The third was a single sentence: The documentation exists. The work of preserving it has been done. What remains is the decision about what to do with it, which I am not in a position to make for you, and which I am giving you the materials to make for yourself.

She put the legal pad down.

The envelope was the standard classification envelope, the kind used for materials that required a specific review authority to open. She sealed the memo inside it. She wrote the classification level on the outside, one level above the NOMAD designation, which would require a review process of the kind that happened when someone was constructing a record for a proceeding or auditing a flagged program, not the kind that happened routinely. She addressed it to the office. She dated it.

She put it in the bottom drawer, at the back, behind the legal pads and the spare pens and the copy of the agency style guide that nobody used but nobody threw away. It would sit there until the drawer was inventoried, which would happen when she left the position, which she did not expect to be soon. She expected the envelope to sit for years. She had written it so that it would still be useful in years, so that the person who opened it would have what they needed to act on it, if they chose to act on it, in a context she could not see from here.

That was all she could do. It was the seventh thing she had done that the institution did not know about, and it was the last one, and she had done it in forty minutes on a Tuesday morning, alone, without ceremony.

She put the legal pad back in the drawer. She closed it.

The work on her desk was the work of the afternoon: three briefings, two routing decisions and one request for a historical records review that she would need to forward to the archivist. She picked up the first briefing. She read the summary paragraph. She made a note in the margin.

Somewhere in the building, the particular sounds of institutional life continued, a printer, a conversation in the corridor, the specific hum of a building that had been running on the same systems for decades and would run on them for decades more. The light through her window was the light of a Tuesday afternoon in whatever season it was, ordinary and sufficient.

She read the next paragraph. She made another note.

In the bottom drawer, behind the legal pads, the envelope sat in the dark and waited for the right kind of inquiry to find it. This might take years. It might take longer. It would wait.

Chapter Thirty: The Quiet After

There is a moment after a great noise stops when the world feels unfinished, as if it is waiting for instructions it will never receive.

The networks slowed first. Not all at once, not dramatically, just a subtle thinning. The hot takes arrived later. The certainty dulled. The outrage learned new targets. News panels moved on because panels always do. A different crisis found the light.

But the archive remained.

Not trending. Not dominant. Just present.

In court filings, footnotes began to appear, dry procedural references to hashes and timestamps that traced back farther than the crisis itself. A judge in Minnesota asked on the record for verification of a detention list and refused to proceed without it. A clerk in Arizona delayed a case by a week because a filing did not pass provenance checks.

Small frictions. Invisible victories.

No one announced them.

In the months that followed, people kept looking for Avril Greenfellow.

They looked in leaked footage and claimed sightings. They analyzed gait and posture. They swore they had heard his voice at a rally that never happened. Conspiracy forums filled with theories that contradicted each other perfectly.

He was dead. He was abroad. He was inside the government. He was the government.

Each claim cancelled the others out.

What people wanted was a spine to grab, a mouth to quote. But mouths could be silenced. Spines could be broken. The absence began to make sense.

The phrase kept appearing in margins, in records, in messages between people who had never met and would never meet. No one was issuing it. No one was maintaining it. It was simply present in the way that true things were present, without needing to be announced because announcing it would have been redundant.

"We don't do authorship anymore," someone wrote in a comment that was shared and reshared without attribution until its origin was untraceable.

Nobody could verify who had written it first. That was the point.

The work changed shape.

There were no operations anymore, not in the old sense. There were custodians. Librarians. Teachers. Quiet professionals who taught verification the way first aid had once been taught, something you hoped you would never need but practiced anyway.

In a community college outside Des Moines, a night class on digital literacy included a unit on chain of custody. No slogans. No politics. Just methods.

"Truth is not a feeling," the instructor said. "It is a process."

Students wrote it down.

In a rural clinic, a nurse kept a printed copy of the Archive Zero fingerprint taped inside a supply cabinet. She had never used it. She was not sure she would know how. But it was there.

That mattered.

The task forces were never formally disbanded. They simply became something else.

Budgets shifted. Language softened. Narrative threats became information resilience. The machinery learned, as machinery always does, to change its vocabulary without changing its appetite.

But it had lost something essential.

It no longer knew where to aim.

She read the brief in silence. The conclusion was careful, bloodless, and accurate.

Recommendation: deprioritize pursuit of individual actors. The phenomenon has decoupled from leadership. Continued focus risks amplification.

She closed the folder.

In the end, the system had learned the wrong lesson too late. Power could not compete with habits.

The people who had carried it did not disappear. They became ordinary.

A family found their way to the coast eventually, not Honduras, not yet, but close enough that the ocean was visible from the window of the place they rented, and the younger girl drew the coastline in her notebook beside the capital city she had memorized from an atlas the previous year. An attorney in a city that was not the city she had left took a case in her first month that she would not have taken before, and won it on a Friday afternoon by the record being what the record was. A man parked a car and walked away from it and became, without effort, the kind of person no one looked for.

The work had made them. It had not consumed them. That was the distinction the machine had never understood: that the people who did this kind of work did not become the work. They passed through it and came out the other side as themselves, changed but not converted, present but not fixed in place.

Avril lived somewhere ordinary.

The place did not matter. It was not a cabin or a bunker or a dramatic exile. It was a room with a window and a table and a routine that did not require explanation.

He worked with his hands now. Physical things. Repairs. Fixes that stayed fixed. He paid cash when he could. He kept his head down not from fear but from completion.

Some mornings, he listened to the radio. Some days, he did not.

He did not check feeds. He did not search his name.

Once, at a hardware store, he saw the phrase scrawled on a bathroom stall:

WE RESIST

It was not his handwriting. It was not anyone he knew.

He washed his hands and left without commenting.

That night, he slept.

Years later, a graduate student writing a dissertation on the collapse of centralized disinformation paused over a footnote.

There was no founding document. No manifesto. No single leader she could cite without qualifiers.

Instead, there were fingerprints. Hashes. Verifications that predated the crisis and outlasted it.

Her advisor frowned. "So who started it?"

The student shook her head. "That is the wrong question."

She underlined a sentence in her draft:

Movements that survive do so by refusing to need their founders.

She saved the file twice.

The phrase never disappeared.

It faded, sharpened, reappeared. Sometimes it was misused. Sometimes it was commercialized. Sometimes it was misunderstood entirely.

But occasionally, quietly, it appeared where it mattered most, in a margin, in a record, in a refusal to accept a convenient lie.

No one could arrest it.

No one could speak for it.

And no one could kill it without killing something much larger than themselves.

The world went on, imperfect and unfinished.

And somewhere within it, without ceremony or permission, the truth remained verifiable.

That was enough.